3 4028 08915 6757
HARRIS COUNTY PUBLIC LIBRARY

LT Western Long W
Long, McKendree R.,
Higher ground /
$25.99   ocn948360748

GROUND

D1572499

WITHDRAWN

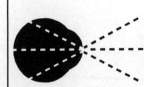

This Large Print Book carries the
Seal of Approval of N.A.V.H.

THE SUPERSTITION GUN TRILOGY

HIGHER GROUND

McKendree Long

WHEELER PUBLISHING
A part of Gale, Cengage Learning

Farmington Hills, Mich • San Francisco • New York • Waterville, Maine
Meriden, Conn • Mason, Ohio • Chicago

GALE
CENGAGE Learning®

Copyright © 2015 by McKendree Long.
The Superstition Gun Trilogy.
Wheeler Publishing, a part of Gale, Cengage Learning.

ALL RIGHTS RESERVED
This is a work of fiction. Names, characters, and incidents are products
of the author's imagination or are used fictitiously and are not to be
construed as real. Any resemblance to actual events, locales,
organizations, or persons, living or dead, is entirely coincidental.
Wheeler Publishing Large Print Western.
The text of this Large Print edition is unabridged.
Other aspects of the book may vary from the original edition.
Set in 16 pt. Plantin.

LIBRARY OF CONGRESS CATALOGING-IN-PUBLICATION DATA

Names: Long, McKendree R., author.
Title: Higher ground / by McKendree Long.
Description: Large print edition. | Waterville, Maine : Wheeler Publishing, 2016. |
   Series: Wheeler Publishing large print western | Series: The superstition gun
   trilogy
Identifiers: LCCN 2016019954 | ISBN 9781410491909 (softcover) | ISBN 1410491900
   (softcover)
Subjects: LCSH: Large type books. | GSAFD: Western stories.
Classification: LCC PS3612.O499 H54 2016 | DDC 813/.6—dc23
LC record available at https://lccn.loc.gov/2016019954

Published in 2016 by arrangement with High Hill Press

Printed in the United States of America
1 2 3 4 5 6 7 20 19 18 17 16

In memory of all the fighters who lost
their lives at the Little Bighorn,
June 25th, 1876.

Dedicated to Mary.

FOREWORD

Canadian Fort, Texas

It seems that fire follows growth as surely as night follows day — or is it the other way around? Since you have stumbled on this humble work, you probably also stumbled through my two previous attempts to chronicle these cycles of destruction and construction in the lives of Thomas 'Dobey' Walls and Jimmy 'Boss' Melton.

You will know then, that I rode with them in The Recent Unpleasantness, as the War of Northern Aggression has now become known in polite circles. You'll know that I have assembled 'facts' from survivors, in some cases years after the actions I'm trying to document. In many cases, memories have faded or key players died, and so I've had to resort to guesswork on some events and conversations.

Because of that, I cannot call this history, but as Historical Fiction, it is as close to the truth as I can tell it. It is certainly *not* Fictional History, as no outcomes have been changed.

Having read *No Good Like It Is* and *Dog Soldier Moon,* you'll also know that a thread running through these stories is a tiny pistol with an unusual serial number, which seems to have a life of its own; an acquaintance even suggested I name this epic "The Superstition Gun Trilogy." I have resisted that temptation, so far.

If you have not tried my previous efforts, you should probably stop now and do that. All of this will make a lot more sense.

William F. 'Buddy' Skipper
March, 1890

■ ■ ■ ■

1870

■ ■ ■ ■

CHAPTER ONE

Dobey

"Sometimes, for an over-taught blind-assed Nigra, you ask some dumb-assed questions."

Big William grinned, then grunted. The wagon he was driving north on Fort Street bounced and clattered over the Kansas Pacific railroad tracks which ran down Front Street in Hays City.

"Yassuh, Boss Melton, but y'all said we come all this way up here, three days from Dodge City, 'cause y'all heard that man Penn was here with the army. We just rode right by that Fort Hays. I just meant, how come we didn't pull up there and look for him. See?"

Jimmy 'Boss' Melton grinned back. Most folks were intimidated by the imposing former Confederate sergeant-major, but he obviously enjoyed the banter with the equally imposing ex-slave. Now he stepped

11

his large sorrel carefully over the tracks and wiped his face with his plaid kerchief. Mid-July in Kansas was hotter than Hades.

"You're the one as don't see, darky. Penn ain't a soldier. If he's here at all, he's a scout, woodcutter, some kinda civilian hanger-on. Maybe a no account wagon driver like you. He'll be in town. You see?"

Dobey Walls, the other horseman bracketing the open wagon, said, "You two don't ever let up, do you? Now listen a minute. What we're gonna do is look up Sheriff Hickok, find out has he seen or heard anything of Penn. And we ought to find the sheriff right around here. Turn right on this next street. We'll pull up behind Paddy Welch's bar over there. Go in the back way."

Melton's mood had suddenly gone dark. "Judas Priest. We can't forget why we's here, not for one minute. Ought to be looking everywhere for that murdering son of a bitch. Liable to stroll in there, find him standing at the bar."

Dobey could almost taste the relish which coated Melton's thoughts of finding Penn. Hell, he felt the same way. Penn was one of two survivors of a gang that had raped his wife and raped and murdered her mother — Melton's wife. Dobey's wife had been shot and left half-dead. Alive, but carrying

12

the rapist's child. Lucky, he thought, still deeply bitter. They'd also killed Dobey's blacksmith, old 'Nacio, and shot off Dobey's mother's arm. It was just her left arm, he thought. Lucky.

That had been almost two years ago. Four of the gang members had already suffered and died at the hands of Dobey and the Boss in their on-again, off-again vengeance ride. Only the leader, Red, and his right hand man, Penn, were left. And it would never be over until they were dead.

Dobey came back to the present. John Walsh's saloon was known by one and all as Paddy Welch's. As the trio approached the back side of the wood structure, they could see a doorway followed by two glass windows.

Muffled gunshots rattled the glass windows. Inside, there was the fast clump of boots running on the wooden floor, and the window closest to them exploded outward as a tall man dove through it. He rolled to his feet and spun to cover Dobey's party with a pair of revolvers.

Dobey said, "Easy, there, Sheriff Hickok — it's me, Dobey Walls. We just came here to see you. How come you didn't use the door?"

Hickok stuck one pistol back in its holster

13

and picked up his hat. "Door swings in, and I's heading out in somewhat of a hurry. Listen, I need to be moving on before half the Seventh Cavalry comes after me."

Dobey said, "Hop in the wagon and pull those buffalo skins over you. Big William, help him, quick. Sheriff, what the hell is going on?"

"Two soldiers jumped me in there, tried to kill me. Nearly did, too. I shot 'em both."

Three minutes later and twenty yards down the street, a half dozen pistol-waving soldiers ran through an open lot and stopped them.

A lanky corporal said, "You see a tall man, white shirt?"

Dobey said, "Man jumped through that window back there, like to scared our horses to death. Waved two pistols at us, then run on up this street and went to the right at the corner."

"He's gone south on Main Street, boys. Get after him. He'll prob'ly duck in Tommy Drum's saloon." Several of the troopers ran off. The corporal and two others stayed. "What y'all doing here?" the corporal asked, waving his pistol vaguely in the direction of the newcomers.

"Just picked up my brother's body," Dobey said. "Looking for the cemetery."

"That him under them skins? Who killed him?" The corporal eased closer to peer into the wagon.

"Ain't nobody kilt him," said Big William. "Bloody flux got him. Red spots all over him, coughing and shitting black blood. My sister been taking care of him, and now these fine gennamens," he nodded at Dobey and the Boss, "they is making me take and bury him. Ain't never no good reward in this life for doing good works. Have to burn my durn buffalo robes once I'm through, if'n I ain't died too. Y'all want to see?"

The soldiers had backed up a step when Big William spat. They now recoiled; one mumbled, "Goddam plague," and the other two crossed themselves.

The corporal said, "You just do what these men tell you, nigger. Y'all need to turn around, go back to Fort Street and turn right. Boot Hill is up that way."

Melton said, "Boot Hill?"

The corporal replied, "It's what these jaybirds here call their cemetery. You can't miss it. And make sure the nigger buries him deep and burns them robes."

Melton, holding a cocked Remington along his leg away from the soldiers, said, "Yes sir." As the soldiers hurried away, he eased the hammer down and slipped the

15

pistol back into its holster.

The wagon creaked and groaned as Big William put it through a tight turn around, and Dobey said, "Well, Sheriff, I can't wait to hear this whole story. Where you want to go?"

Hickock pushed the covers off his upper body, but stayed low. "My boarding house, first. Need my rifle and some more ammunition. And then Boot Hill. Ain't a bad place to hide out for the night and a good place to defend, do it come to that. We'll talk there. Boarding house is on the way. And I ain't sheriff here no more."

"Finally out of the law business?" Dobey asked, as they rode north on Fort Street.

"Not exactly," said Hickok. "I'm still deputy U.S. Marshal. Pull over here."

Dobey said, "You'd best stay hid. Tell me what you need and where it is."

"Hold on a minute," Melton said. "We been on the edge of a gunfight for the last little bit, over somebody I ain't even ever met."

"Sorry," Dobey said. "Bad manners. This here is J.B. Hickok, mostly known as Wild Bill. Marshal, that's my partner, Jimmy Melton — mostly known as 'Boss.' I 'spect you remember Big William from last September."

16

Melton said, "Heard of you. Nice to meet you. How bad you hit?"

Hickok sat up and said, "Hit. Who, me? Where?"

Melton said, "They's blood on your boot. Maybe you cut it when you missed the door."

Big William pushed on the foot brake and spun around into the wagon bed. He helped Hickok get the heavy robes off his legs, then squatted to look at the wound.

"Ain't bleeding much, Cap'n Dobey. Looks like a ball went in below the knee and come out'n his boot down low. We best get somewhere's I can give it a better look."

Hickok said, "We'll do that on Boot Hill. Dobey, my room's top of the stairs, front side. It ain't locked. Winchester's in the corner, sort of behind the dresser. There's boxes in the top left drawer. Forty-four rim-fires and some paper cartridges for my Colts. A tin of caps and a pistol capper. Oh, and a box with foreign writing on it that says 'Nine millimeter.' Pinfires. Pistol's under the pillow. Lemme think here. Bring that bottle on the table . . . and they's a carpet bag under the bed you can throw all that in."

CHAPTER TWO

Dobey

Long shadows stabbed at them from two lone trees to the west as they finally pulled off Fort Street into the burial grounds of Boot Hill.

"Be dark soon," said Dobey. "Let's get as far off the road as we can, find a flat spot and start digging. Got to have a respectable mound for my poor dead brother come morning, else the army will be hard after us."

"First things first," said Melton. "I need the marshal here to tell me is Penn down there in that town."

Hickok pushed the heavy fur robes off again, sat up, and said, "No sir." As the wagon bounced and creaked over the rocky ground to the back of the small rise, Hickok took out the whiskey, took a swig, then recorked it and tossed it to Melton. "Y'all just missed him. It was him 'bout got me kilt back there."

Melton took a swig and passed the bottle to Dobey. "Come again?"

"Give me a minute," Hickok said, as Big William halted the team and set the brake. "Y'all watch out. I need to stretch and piss afore anybody shows up here, though ain't no one likely to come up here this late."

Dobey and Melton unsaddled and Big William unhitched the team while the lawman limped off to relieve himself.

"Water and feed 'em, Big William. We'll get more grain and water in the morning before we push on. We'll take turns digging tonight, with one of us watching the road. We don't need to go too deep, but it does need to look real," Dobey said, unstrapping the pick and shovel from the wagon.

Hickok returned, buttoning up his plaid trousers. "Lemme have that pick," he said. "I'll start. I'm just real happy this ain't my grave we're digging."

Dobey passed the pick to the marshal and said, "Tell us about Penn, and what the hell happened down there."

"Last time you was here, I tole Big William that Penn was likely to come back. Well, he did, so I heard last week. I been asking around, trying to get a fix on him. Being careful, I thought, but he got wind of it somehow. He jumped a train toward Abilene this morning, but not before he set them two soldiers to get me. Probably paid 'em a few dollars, or bought 'em a drink. Who knows? All I know is, I'm having a drink with Paddy there in his bar, and the big sergeant, Lonergan, Lanahan, something like that, he slips up behind me, gets a headlock on me. My arms are sticking straight out to the sides, see, and he's a strong one, bigger'n me even. I can't do much, and he says right in my ear, 'Looking for Penn, are we? We'll just put an end to that, Mister Lawman.' Well, I saw in the mirror he had another soldier with him, and that one's pulling a Remington out of his blouse. I jack my legs against the bar and push and we land on the floor, him on his back and me on top with my back to him. I'm twisting to beat hell, finally get my right hand to where I can grab a Colt, but before I can shoot, the little one puts his pistol muzzle against my head . . ." Hickok paused for effect, "and snapped a cap on me. Misfired, big as you please. Else this hole would be for me, sure as God made apples."

Melton took the pick from Hickok and handed him the bottle. Hickok took a swallow, then started to finish his story.

Big William stopped him. "You go right

on talking, Mister Marshal, but I needs to pull off that boot and look at your leg."

Everyone paused. Dobey said, "You're supposed to be watching the road."

Big William said, "Ain't nobody coming, Cap'n. Ain't gonna come either, after that story I told 'em." He giggled, then yanked off Hickok's boot. "The leg ain't too bad, I think. I'll clean it up. Y'all go on and talk."

The marshal shrugged and said, "Anyways, I was able to put a ball through the little one's arm, so he drops his pistol. Put the next one in his body, so he yells, 'Oh, shyte,' and goes down. Then I get the gun upside the big un's leg and get off another shot. He started screaming, 'My knee, my knee', and let me go, so I excused myself and eased right on out through that window pane. And there y'all were, waiting outside to save me. Ain't no way I can ever thank you enough, either."

Melton put down the pick and said, "Shovel this out a while, Dobey," then bent to look at Hickok's leg.

Hickok said, "Afore you start, Dobey, if you'll hand me my carpet bag I'll reload this Colt."

Big William looked up at Melton and said, "Funny looking wound, Boss. What you make of it?"

21

Melton made a face. "Weren't bad enough to stop his feet from stinking. Looks like the ball went down the leg, under the skin, and out above the ankle. It ain't bad. Who shot you?"

It was Hickok's turn to make a face. "They didn't get off a shot. Must have been me. Probably through his kneecap and into my own leg. Can we keep that fact amongst us girls?"

Big William laughed in his deep rumble. "Yassuh, Mister Marshal. Way it went in, I thought maybe that's what happened. Now if'n you pass me that bottle, I be putting a taste on your leg."

"Do what? You gone loco?" Hickok held the bottle against his chest.

"Doc Thomason, he says always put some on a bad cut or a bullet hole. Says it kindly like cleans it out good."

Hickok looked dubious. "We ain't got much left as it is."

"Doc say it don't take much. Just enough so it burns. Say that means it's working, and it might keep your leg from turning green and having to come off."

Hickok jerked erect and thrust the bottle to Big William. "Here. Go ahead. Use it all. And hurry."

■ ■ ■ ■

Big William

Big William watched as Hickok woke to the smell of wood smoke and coffee. The crackle of Big William's little cook fire mixed with the sizzle and pop of bacon frying. The lawman sat up and stretched. And scratched. And groaned.

Big William grinned at him. "Little early for you, Mister Marshal? Cap'n Dobey done rode back down into town, see can he get us some feed and news."

Marshal Hickok pulled on his boots. "Judas priest, man, it's barely dawn. Where's the big one?"

Big William said. "Boss Melton? He gone to do his business." He nodded to some bushes thirty yards away. "They is a catalogue under the wagon seat, if'n you need some paper yourself."

Hickok poured himself some coffee. "Maybe after he comes back. Listen here. Last time I seen you, you told me Dobey was all messed up in his head 'cause his woman had a baby from this Penn fellow attacking her, right?"

"Nossir. What I said was, it was Penn's boss, a man name of Red, he's the one as

23

ruint Miz Honey and give her that baby boy. Penn was the one as took Miz Honey's mother by force, and then killed her. Him and another man. And Miz Honey's mother was Boss Melton's woman."

Melton returned and got some coffee himself. "Morning, Marshal."

"Mornin' yourself, Boss. I'm just trying to figure out the difference in how Dobey's acting now, vicey-versey how he was last time I seen him," Hickok said, strapping on his two revolvers. "He don't seem so messed up over his wife and the baby and all."

"Couple of things happened, I guess. First off, turns out he'd made another baby his own self, one he didn't know about. Me and him stopped overnight at a farm on the way home in '65 and had an interesting evening with a couple of widow women. One he's with had a little boy. She died, but the one I was with brung the boy out to see did his daddy want him."

Big William said, "Second thing was Boss Melton here got on Cap'n Dobey about how he was treating Miz Honey, even before the surprise baby showed up. Said he wished his woman had come through it carrying a baby, and alive. Ever'body felt that way, but couldn't nobody say nothing 'cept the Boss. I mean, nothing the Cap'n would listen to."

Hickok nodded. "Sort of took him off his high ground. I mean, I know he ain't exactly cheerful about things yet, but I could see he won't be in that, 'Why me, Lord?' sort of way no more."

Melton poured out his coffee dregs. "Dobey's a good man. Best I ever worked with. He was messed up a while but he's past it now. 'Bout as normal as he could be. It helps, watching Honey raise those two boys as if she'd had 'em both willing, and with Dobey."

Big William handed both men tin plates of bacon and fry bread. "See, Mister Marshal, they also got a little girl that they did have together, and that helps too. Dobey's a good daddy, now he got his head on right."

Dobey rejoined them minutes later and traded Big William a bag of oats and a bundle of hay for a plate of food and a cup of coffee.

"One of them soldiers died this morning. Other one's knee is ruint. We're all right, though, I think. I told folks nobody had come this way. Told some others I heard the marshal had rode out toward Fort Dodge." Dobey paused. "Just where do you want us to take you, Marshal?"

Hickok said, "There's a woodcutter's camp a few miles north of here. They think highly of me. Maybe get a bite to eat there, then take a trail east maybe eight miles to Big Creek Station. Y'all can refill your water barrel there, and I'll catch a train on further east. To Abilene. See can I find our back-stabbing friend Penn again."

"You might want to stay on there a while," Dobey said. "I heard this morning that the Seventh Cavalry is heading for the Carolinas soon. 'Peace-keeping Reconstruction Duty' is what they called it."

"That's a good thing," said the lanky law-man, twisting his mustache tips. "I do worry about backshooters."

As they approached Big Creek Station, Dobey said, "I think we'll leave our horses here with Big William and the wagon and take the train to Abilene with you, Marshal. In case Penn is still there."

Hickok said, "If he's there, I could just kill him for you. Save you the trip."

Melton shook his head and said, "No. That won't do. He's mine."

Dobey said, "Right. Who don't know that? Big William, we'll see you in a couple days. Keep that big-assed shotgun nearby, but put this pistol in your pocket." He handed the big black man a cut-down Navy Colt from his saddlebag.

Hickok looked behind the wagon seat. "I been meaning to ask you about this shotgun — you mind do I handle it? What the hell you got here?"

As Hickok picked it up, Melton said, "Used to be mine. Thieving old darky borrowed it and won't give it back. It's a ten gauge five shooter. We keep it loaded with three buckshot on top of a seventy-five caliber ball, each chamber. That way he can hit something the size of the wagon at close range. Some of the time. We call it the Avenging Angel."

Big William gave Hickok a rueful grin. "Boss Melton just be messing with you, Mister Marshal. I didn't borrow it. No sir. He made me take it. Said I couldn't hit nothing noways without it. See, it was before I was give these spectacles. But ain't nobody gonna borrow nothing from Boss Melton less'n he wants 'em to."

Hickok replaced the Colt revolving shotgun carefully. "I doubt that you have to do much except point it at somebody. Staring into that barrel is like looking into a cave. I can testify to that."

Melton swung in the saddle to stare at the lawman. "And when did that happen?"

"Last time he was here with Dobey. We almost got crossways, and all of a sudden

27

Big William swings that thing towards me, and I'm looking into the mouth of Hell itself. Old fool didn't realize he was up against Wild Bill hisself, most feared lawman in Kansas. I near shit my pants."

Big William didn't need the pistol or the Avenging Angel during his stay at Big Creek Station. Two days after they left, Dobey and Boss Melton stepped off the west-bound train, grimy, sweat-soaked, and irritable. Penn had simply passed through Abilene for parts unknown. They watered up and headed home, but Dobey insisted they stop by Boot Hill again. There they found a nice wooden marker on the grave they'd dug.

Thom. M. Walls, Capt. CSA
James Melton, Srgt. Major, CSA
JULY 17 1870
FLUX DONE WHAT BULLETTS COULDN'T DO
R.I.P.

"I got the man at the gun store to do it," Dobey said, grinning. "Maybe it'll head off those Pinkertons. Wish he had spelled bullets right."

CHAPTER THREE

Penn

As the stage labored up the steep grade, the shotgun guard yelled down to tell the occupants that they were about a half-hour outside of Santa Fe. The six miserable passengers began to yawn, groan, and knuckle their eyes.

Penn stretched as best he could in the cramped space and glanced at the others. A middle-aged Mexican couple with an older woman, all well-dressed. Husband, wife, mother-in-law, Penn guessed. Fancy-pants, all of 'em. Drunk Army captain who'd snored most of the trip, and a mining engineer coming back from a visit to the East.

And Penn. He'd dreaded this trip from the start, when he set out from Abilene to try to find Red and warn him about the Texans looking for him. It had been worse than he expected.

He nodded to the engineer as he dug his cold cigar from his shirt pocket. The rain had become steady since dawn, but with no breeze the passengers were protected from most of the wet.

The engineer grinned. "We finally get out of the dust, and then we make our own smoke." He struck a match to re-light Penn's stub of a cigar, then fired up a fresh one of his own. "Still and all, it's kindly nice to be warm and dry on a dark day such as this."

Penn nodded in agreement. "And that's a fact," he said. "I'd heap ruther chew my arm off than make a long ride on horseback in mess like this. You know much about this here Santy Fe we're coming to?"

"Used to live here. What you need to know?"

Penn took off his hat and stuck his head out to catch some rain, then wiped his face with his kerchief as he thought about his answer. He couldn't just say, "Some tough hombres want to kill me and my old partner, and now Wild Bill Hickok is helping 'em." The engineer puffed and waited.

Penn said, "Know a man that come here a while back. Might still be here. Might have kept going. Goes by Red, mostly, on account of his hair and beard. Might be some

30

other folks is looking to hurt him. Thought I'd let him know."

The engineer squinted in thought a few seconds, then said, "Can't say as anyone comes to mind. They's a post office and the stage ticket office, might help you. Town marshal, of course, and most folks eat at Watson's Café. Chili's right good there. Anybody can point it out, if'n you're able to find someone who speaks English." His voice rose as he cut his eyes toward the Mexican family, who'd been quietly conversing in Spanish. The captain snored on.

As the stage clattered and jingled to a halt, Penn pulled his bedroll from under his feet and took his slicker from it. He re-wrapped the bedroll around his Spencer carbine, tied the roll, then struggled into the slicker, bumping the officer awake.

"Where the hell are we?" The soldier slurred, as he opened one eye.

"California," Penn said, as he stepped out and down. He winked at the engineer as the shotgun guard tossed down his saddlebags.

The soldier muttered, "Damn. That was a fast trip," and went back to sleep.

The ticket office couldn't help Penn and the post office was closed, but the marshal was in, and was helpful.

"Set a spell," the lawman said. "Help yourself to some of that coffee. You're the second person come looking for this feller, if'n he's the same identical one. Sounds like it. Young girl name of Consuela come up from San Vicente hunting him some time back, but he ain't here. You looking to make bounty on him?"

That woke Penn up. "Come again?"

The lawman said, "You don't look like no Pinkerton to me, but then I ain't seen all that many. Are you an Agency man?"

Penn shook his head, still wary.

"Didn't think so. Well, I got paper on this Red feller. Pretty good reward. He shot up Watson's place, kilt two Pinkertons. Watson thinks he stung him with some pellets as he took off, after Miz Watson poured some hot stew on his head. Talk to the girl. She says he showed up in San Vicente and she worked for him when he run a cantina his-self. Then he give up on running the cantina, sudden-like, and just run off."

Penn said, "So he left and came back this way?"

"She don't know. She was guessing, since she knowed he was here before. Might be he didn't tell her about the dust-up he had here, and the Pinkertons and all."

Penn shrugged. "Might be. And might be

32

we talking about two different Reds. See, the one I'm looking for is kind of scrawny, don't talk much. Mean-spirited."

The lawman shook his head. "Naw. Not the same man. One that was here was pretty good-sized and a real charmer. Watson said he could talk a bird out'n a tree, but it's pretty clear he could be mean."

Penn drained his coffee and stood. "Well, you can probably tear that reward paper up. That was Red Dodd. I knowed him too. He crossed back to Texas and some Comanches caught him and a small party in the open. Nigger cavalry run off the injins, but that Red was shot full of arrows. I know that was him 'cause he always carried an old town marshal badge, and they found it on him."

The lawman slammed his fist on the desk. "By God, that's him. Watson talked about that badge too. Well, I reckon I can wire the Pinkertons to forget about that one. Ain't likely they'll wanna pay that bounty to no Comanches. You moving on now?"

"I'll go by Watson's, get some grub and see has he seen my man. Maybe ask the girl did she see somebody like him in Saint Vincent, or whatever you called it." Penn paused in the door. "Thanks for the coffee and the talk. Which way to Watson's?"

The marshal pointed. "Down thataway. Far side of the *zocalo.*"

"The what?"

"*Zocalo?* The town square."

Consuela had an easy walk that would stir a dead man, even if she hadn't been pretty. Her smile held a promise for every man she served, and each blink of her dark eyes was deliberate and slow. Penn felt some stirrings himself.

She placed the bowl of chili in front of him then placed both hands on the table and bent forward to give him a glimpse of her melons.

"You want some coffee, Senor? Or maybe something else?" Innocent smile. Reddish hair. Full lips. She wet them with a flick of her tongue. Freckles? Irish daddy, Penn thought. This is getting out of hand.

"Why didn't you just bring the damn coffee with the food?" He gave her his hard stare. The scary one.

She shrugged, giving him a better glimpse of those globes. "Because I think maybe you like to watch me walk."

As she swayed back to the kitchen, Penn couldn't help breaking into a wide grin. This one's trouble. She paused at another table, looked back at him and gave him that slow blink.

She brought the coffee and sat, pulling her chair close. He felt her toe against the back of his ankle. He said, "This chili is mighty good, but I don't know if men come here for it, or just to watch you sashay around."

"Men need to dream. And sometimes a poor senorita needs a little extra *dinero*. Like when a shit-head like our Senor Red runs off without paying."

Penn pushed a small silver coin to her. "Go on."

She got serious. "Some soldiers got sick on our food. Their coronel said he would hang Red, so he run. Right then. He got on his horse and lit out. I didn't know where. I waited in his room a few days, then brung his traps and come here looking. He didn't leave much. Some dirty clothes, which I washed. Hand mirror, silver comb and razor. A little pistola under his ticking. A nice cloth satchel. But I know he had some dinero too, and it wasn't there, so he must have had it on him. I found out he come from here when he come to San Vicente, so here I am."

"But he didn't come this way. You seen any Pinkertons?"

"No. Why? I know of them. Special *policia,* no?" She touched his hand.

He said, "Police. Yeah. Well, they will come. We got to spread the word that old Red is dead. Get 'em off his trail, but see has they heard any more on his whereabouts. I mean, if'n you wants to go with me looking for him."

"Oh, si. Si, Senor. This I do want. You got money? For us, I mean?"

"Not no great deal of it. How come?"

Consuela said, "These gringos I work for, they has some. You help me get away, I can get it."

"We gotta kill 'em, or can you just steal it?"

"I can get their *muchacho* Button to tell me where it's hid. He's in heat, sniffing around little Consuelita." She blinked. When her eyes opened, they were cut away toward Button, a teenage boy clearing a table by the far wall. She blinked slowly again and was once more staring into Penn's face.

Those damn eyes. "Why don't' ya take me right now, show me where you're gonna perform this miracle, and let me see what that boy is sniffing after. Then I'll get us a couple of horses."

■ ■ ■ ■

It was dusk and the drizzle had started again, this time with gusting wind and thunder. Penn stood by the stable door, watching sheet lightning dance across the horizon.

Whoever ran the stable must have gone to Watson's for supper, so Penn had picked out two mares from the five horses stabled inside the barn. A small Appaloosa for Consuela and a bigger roan for himself.

"Probably belong to somebody. Might be better than them in the corral out back. Damn sure easier to saddle up in here than out there. And drier." He said to himself.

Using the same logic, he'd chosen saddles, blankets, and tack from a rack marked 'No Sale.' He hoped the girl got here with the money before the liveryman finished eating. He might dispute Penn's choices, and Penn hated knife work. He just hated disputes and paying for stuff even more.

"Knife work is just plain messy. And tricky, compared to gun work," he said.

"Que?"

She was just outside the door, under the eave. She stepped in carefully and looked around the darkening barn. She wore loose pants and a man's shirt and hat, and carried a cloth satchel.

"You 'bout scared the piss outta me, girl. Whose clothes you wearing?"

"The *muchacho's.* Button Watson's. Who were you talking to? You scared me too. Ah. You were talking to yourself."

"You got the money?"

"Si, I got it." She patted the satchel.

"You hurt the boy?"

"Didn't have to. Took him to my room, give him some mescal. Played with his pizzle, put my tongue on his ear. He told me ever' thing. Said he loved me. He's passed out naked in my room, but we got to *vamonos, muy pronto.* Here's your cut." She pulled a sheaf of bills from the valise.

Penn counted it. "A hundred dollars? You said they had real money. *Mucho dinero,* you said."

"Not so much as I thought. You know, maybe they had some hid that the *muchacho* didn't know about."

Penn drew his old Navy Colt and said, "I'll shoot you right in the gut, leave you screaming and dying, you lying whore. Give it up. All of it." He cocked the revolver and pointed it at her belly.

"You won't kill me here. They'll be all over you. And that lawman likes my favors." Her eyes blazed defiance.

"You listen, missy. I'll tell 'em you poxed me, and tooken this money off me. But it won't matter at all to your darling little bottom 'cause you'll be dead as a red brick."

She changed before his eyes. "Listen to little Consuelita, *jefe.* That boy wakes up, or old man Watson goes to his stash, they'll know where the money came from. Jus' calm down or we both lose out. Here, take my half, but let's ride. Before we're caught." She drew another handful of bills from the satchel and shoved them at him. "Three hundred's better than none."

"Three hundred? Your cut was gonna be twice mine? You little vixen, you got more balls than most men."

"I did the work. I took the risk. But now we just split it, si?"

"We don't split nothing, you lying cheat. You're lucky I don't just kill you. I'm taking it all and both horses. I'm gonna tie you and gag you and if you make any fuss I'll burn this barn down right on you. Go sit against that post. Move!" He motioned with his pistol, then turned to stuff the money into a pocket on his slicker, hanging from his saddle horn.

He heard her say, "Si, Senor, jus' don' hurt me none. All right?" And then he heard the double click of a pistol being cocked. He spun to cover her as she fired.

Her bullet hit his brass trigger guard and glanced down to take off his middle finger at the lower joint. His pistol chain-fired, five chambers going off at once. It bucked out of his mangled hand.

Four of his bullets missed her. The fifth ball hit her in the throat. She dropped the sawed-off Smith and Wesson, grabbed her throat and sat down, gurgling.

Penn stood stunned for a moment. "A flame-over," he muttered. "Forgot to grease the chambers. A damn flame-over." His pistol had landed in a steaming pile of fresh droppings. He picked up the little Smith and Wesson and jammed it in his holster, then yanked off his kerchief and wrapped his bleeding hand.

"Bitch," he said, and kicked her. She fell backward still clutching her throat with both hands, the bright blood spraying through her fingers. He pulled on his slicker and untied both horses. As he mounted the roan, Consuela's arms flopped out to her sides. She stopped twitching and her eyes rolled back.

"Yeah," he said, looking down at her. "Gimme that blink now." Pulling the Appaloosa, he rode out the back through the corral and into the wet night.

Henry Watson

The marshal scratched his head and then his butt as he explained the crime scene to Henry Watson and several other town folks the morning after the robbery.

"Somebody shot her in the neck and left a Navy Colt in that pile of shit there, Mr. Watson. Trigger guard's bent and it's empty. Blood all over it. And she had over two thousand dollars on her. Paper money in her garter belt and a sack of coins in her bag there."

Watson rubbed his chin. "Had to of been that stranger. She talked to him a long time in the cafe, then left with him. She got Button drunk, busted his cherry and got him to tell where our stash was hid. They must of come to odds with one another here. Less'n you can catch him, we're out about three hundred dollars."

"Yessir. I'm right sorry. Old Jim here at the barn is out two good horses with saddle and tack too. One of 'em belonged to the judge. The one as did it is hurt, though. When Old Jim come in this morning there was part of a finger a-laying right there," he pointed, "but when I come in with my dog, she grabbed it and run off. See, I hadn't fed

her yet. Anyways, some of the boys is getting their horses and guns and we'll get after
him. If we can find his tracks behind all this
rain."

CHAPTER FOUR

Penn

Penn found his way into the stage road easily enough, even in the rain and the dark, but ran out of steam after what seemed like fifty miles.

"Probably closer to twenty," he mumbled aloud. "No matter, I got to rest and eat. And old Red is just on his own. Ain't no way I can warn him if I can't find out where he is."

As dawn broke, he came to a way station for the stage line. Just stop long enough to get some hot coffee, he thought. Maybe trade off the little Appaloosa. Damn station agent's gonna report me, though. Just have to put him down. Might be some more money for the taking, though. And food.

He tied off the horses by the water trough in front of the cabin, looked around, and drew Consuela's little Smith and Wesson. He went in the front door fast and ready.

The cabin was empty. A bunk looked slept in and there was a tin cup holding an inch of warm coffee on the table, but no sign of anyone.

"Yo," he shouted. "Anybody home?"

Nothing. Dead still.

"Don't make me come find you. Just come on in here and show your face. It'll be fine. You make me hunt you, I'll kill you when I find you. You come on in, I won't hurt you none."

He thought he heard a door slam outside somewhere. He moved quickly through the eating area and out a side door and made a dash for the barn. It was empty. Relay horses milled around in the corral after he stirred them with his little run, but there wasn't a soul in the barn. Penn started back to the cabin but changed direction when he noticed the privy on the other side of the back lot. As he approached it he heard horses running and turned to see both of his mounts disappear into the brush on a small hill across the stage trail. There was a rider on his roan.

"You thieving son of a bitch, you bring them horses back," he yelled as he ran after them. He had just gotten to the front corner of the cabin when there was the boom of a rifle shot. Dirt flew up a step to his right,

44

and smoke blossomed from the small hill. He broke left and ducked into the front door again just as a second shot splintered the door frame.

Penn sat on the floor gasping for breath and wondered what else could go wrong—and then realized the agent was probably shooting at him with his own Spencer carbine. And there was probably only a hundred rounds of .56-.50 Spencer in his saddle bags.

He broke open the little Smith and Wesson he'd taken off that Mexican witch. Five rounds left. Jesus.

"Hey," he yelled. "Where was you hiding? And what's your name?"

"Livengood. I'm M.C. Livengood, station master, and I won't hiding nowhere. I was in the privy doing my morning business like a honest man, 'til I heard you in there raising sand and a-threatening me. Is they two of you?"

"Naw, Mister Livengood, it's only me." Shit. Why'd I tell him that? "I'm sorry I acted that way. What do you want now? How can I make this right?"

"I'll tell you what you can do. You can toss your pistol out front and come on out and lay on your belly. I'll come tie your thieving ass up and then decide whether to let you ride on off to the east on the morning stage from Santy Fe. Or maybe send you on to Santy Fe to stand trial for attempted robbery."

Penn yelled, "That ain't no choice, Mister Livengood. How 'bout I just grab one of them horses in the corral and ride away?"

"Try it. I ain't much of a shot with a carbine, but I can surely hit a horse. Iffen I has to kill every durn horse in my remuda to stop you, I will. Now, the other thing is, you could take that shotgun which I know you've noticed by now, and you could just charge me. Me and this nice carbine you give me, and it just topped off. You want choices? Wait 'til about midmorning when that stage comes in from Santy Fe. I'll have help then. We'll give you some choices."

Penn had not noticed the shotgun. It was an old double-barrel hanging over the front door. He grabbed it and tore out the back door, uphill past the privy.

The first shot went just over his shoulder and blew a hole in the privy door. Penn spun and fired one barrel of the old gun toward the smoking hilltop, then started chugging uphill again. He thought, I hope that ain't birdshot, and I ain't got no reloads for this. Best be more careful with my shots.

Penn cut left toward a large rock outcrop on the slope. The next shot tore by his right ear. He's getting better, he thought. As he started to dive behind the outcrop, he yelled, "Made it!"

He didn't. A big Spencer slug hit the boulder and sent rock and lead splinters into his left thigh. He screamed and went down.

Choking for breath, he surveyed his situation. Thirty to forty yards of clear hillside in every direction to the next cover, and he wasn't sure he could run. Damn leg might be broke. Old Livengood was getting better with each shot, and the morning stage was coming with help. For Livengood.

Penn peeled off his slicker and made sure the stolen cash was deep in one pocket and the little pistol was in the other. He rolled up the slicker and shoved it up under a ledge on the back of the boulder. He muttered, "Y'all wait for me, you hear?" Without exposing himself, he fired the other barrel in Livengood's general direction, and got two quick return shots spanging off the boulder.

"Hey, Livengood. You know I'm out of ammunition here, and I'm hit. I quit. I'm coming down. Don't shoot me no more."

■ ■ ■ ■

Penn lay on the ground between the cabin and the water trough. His leg had almost stopped bleeding, but it hurt like blue blazes.

"Ain't you gonna do nothing for me? You shot me."

M.C. Livengood sat on the low stoop in the cabin doorway, Penn's Spencer across his lap. Drinking coffee. His third cup. He'd made Penn kneel on the cabin floor while he brewed it. He tossed away the dregs now, and stood. And stretched. Penn hated him.

"That was pure cruel, making me get on my knees in there."

Livengood said, "What's your name anyways, thief?"

"Ah . . ." Penn paused, "I didn't say."

"Well, Mister No-Name, it ain't like I'm out to help you feel nice exactly. But that ain't Christian, is it? Since you can't seem to just enjoy this fine morning sunshine, maybe you'd like a bath and some whiskey? Fried aigs and a side of bacon? Coffee?"

Penn's stomach growled. "You hear that? I ain't ate since noon yesterday. You ain't even give me no water."

"How 'bout I just put a bullet in your

murderous, thieving ass? Save the county a trial and save me listening to your whining. Listen here, my boy lives with me, mostly. He's supposed to be on this next stage from Santy Fe. When I gets some help, we'll tie you up, and clean you up, and maybe patch you up. 'Til then, I ain't getting near you. Don't care if your laig falls off and you mortify. Or starve." Livengood poured another cup of coffee from the pot inside the door and sat down again.

"I notice you has a empty holster, Mister No-Name. Did you lose your pistol up on the hill?"

"Naw," said Penn. "Somebody shot off my finger yesterday. Made me drop it. Back in Santa Fe."

"Iffen my boy comes in, one of us will take you and them horses back to Santy Fe. That little Appaloosa looks mighty much like Shorty Long's pony. The roan could be old man Attleboro's."

The stage thundered in before noon and the agent's boy was on it, but it mattered little to Penn. A posse searching for Penn was with the stage. By late afternoon he was back in Santa Fe, in the county jail. His leg really hurt. After he told them his name was Robbins they finally fed him.

CHAPTER FIVE

Henry Watson

Henry Watson sat with his youngest son Button in the crowded cantina which sometimes served as Santa Fe's county court. He thought the crowd was a lot more agitated than usual. The big room was not exactly smoke-filled yet, but it was working on it. It wasn't too early, maybe nine of the morning, but Button was still sleepy-eyed. He'd come in late from shooting prairie dogs, the carne in Watson's chili con carne.

"How is it we're supposed to know this feller, Daddy?" Button paused to yawn again. "Robbins, right? I don't remember him none."

Watson said, "You ain't met him afore this week. But we think he was maybe looking for that man Red that tried to kill us, you and me and Mama, what, maybe two years back? If it is, we need to get word to Buck and his friends over to Texas. And I'm pretty

50

sure he stole money from us. Easy now, here comes the judge."

The judge's table was set up in the back corner, away from windows and near the kitchen. A slender red-headed man in a black suit pushed out of the kitchen holding a tin cup. He withdrew a Dragoon Colt from his shoulder holster and placed it on the table.

"Coffee," he said, to no one in particular, holding up the cup before taking a sip.

"Yeah, right," snorted one of the bystanders. Several others snickered.

The town marshal moved closer to the judge's table and banged on the bar with the butt of his short shotgun. "Y'all ease up now. Santa Fe Court is now in session. This here is Judge John Huffman Attleboro, as if y'all didn't know, and it's his court today."

The marshal paused as the crowd settled in with a lot of muttering and scraping of chairs on the wooden floor, then went on with his bailiff duties.

"First case is Billy Edmonds. Public drunkenness, vagrancy, and making a disturbance. He called my girlfriend a whore, your Honor."

Edmonds stepped forward with a big grin. He peeled off his slouch hat and said, "Good morning, Judge Addlebrain! Nice to see you again!"

Attleboro peered at him over his spectacles "And thirty good mornings to you. Who's next?"

A deputy led the stunned Edmonds away and the marshal shoved a shackled prisoner forward.

"Sean Robbins, so he says, your Honor. Murder, robbery, stole two horses with saddles and tack. Threatened M.C. Livengood, agent at the Twenty-mile Station."

The judge said, "Murdered who? Robbed what? Just for the record, I mean."

"Murdered Senorita Consuela Valdez, Judge. And on top of them two horses we caught him with, yours and Shorty's, we think he stole maybe three hundred dollars from Mister Henry Watson there." The marshal pointed at Watson. "Though we didn't find none on him."

Watson nodded and said, "Morning, Judge."

The judge gave him a finger-wave and said, "Henry."

The accused sighed and hung his head. Judge Attleboro gave him a probing stare and said, "What do you plead?"

"Not guilty, Judge. That Mexican whore tried to rob and kill me. Shot my gun outta my hand and it went off. It was a accidental

52

self-defense killing. Hell, she shot off my finger. And I didn't get no money. You heard the marshal. And I only took them horses 'cause she said they was hers, and I run cause I heard maybe some lawman was sweet on her . . ."

The marshal broke in. "Your Honor. Your Honor, I'd like to add a charge of public disturbance on him too. He just called my girlfriend a whore, same as Billy Edmonds did."

The judge rubbed his face. "She's dead, Bob. We got to move on."

"Yessir, Judge. Well, he also might have been looking for that man Red Dodd who was through here in '68. Same one as shot up Hank Watson's place and kilt them Pinkertons."

"Nossir!" shouted the accused man. "No sir, your Honor. I's looking for an entire different Red. The one y'all want is dead, killed by Comanches over in the Llano Estacado. I knowed him, but ain't never had no dealings with him. And here I am, shot twice, and all I did was try to defend myself against that greaser slut, uh, girl, and that so-called agent who took my horses and shot me with my own carbine. This ain't right!"

"Your horses? Yours? I've heard enough,"

the judge said. "Five years in Territorial Prison." He banged the table with his pistol. "Court is closed."

The crowd noise exploded with chatter and the rattle of chairs. As the marshal led him away, the prisoner yelled above the din. "Territorial Prison? Where's that at?"

The judge finally smiled. "Why, Mister Robbins, it's under construction. Right down the street. So — for the foreseeable future, it's the same Santa Fe county jail you been resting in. Under the total control of our very own 'greaser' Town Marshal, Roberto 'Bob' Gonzales. Enjoy your stay." He shoved the Dragoon back in its underarm holster and said, "Bar's open."

Watson faced his son. "I'll go help mama get a batch ready for the midday crowd. You take and ride straightaway out to Twentymile Station and give that cabin a good going-over, see did maybe this man Robbins hide our money in it whilst he was penned up inside. Or could be old Livengood found it in Robbin's saddlebags and kept it hisself. Be back in time to kill us some more meat."

Button said, "Yessir. Anything else?"

"Yeah. Avoid loose women."

CHAPTER SIX

Annette

"You know we needs to leave, Miz Annette. I ain't comfortable in the same vicinity of Doc and Buck together. You know I worry Doc will take slight at something, and call Buck out on it. And Buck ain't no mankiller. Everybody knows that." Junebug accepted another sack, this one full of canned goods, but stopped short of stowing it in the wagon to stare into Annette Walls Balliett's worried face.

Annette shrugged and thought, In her shoes I'd do the same. Probably. She picked up a sack of vegetables and handed it up. "You know don't nobody want y'all to leave. Tell me again where you're heading."

"Buck says they's two forts maybe halfway tween here and Fort Worth. Griffin and Richardson." Junebug arched her back and knuckled it. "We figger one or t'other might need a whorehouse and saloon. Bow-Legs

Annie has fallen out with Melton's sister, 'cause Annie won't sell no darkies a poke. She'll help me start the business. And we'll get this wagon back to you soon as we can."

The two women were inside the adobe walls of Balliett's Post, the big mud fort of the tiny trading outpost also known as Canadian Fort. It sat along the South Canadian River, in the lonely, windy, northern regions of the Texas Panhandle.

"Miles from anywhere," Annette said.

"Say what?" Junebug responded. "We ain't gonna be near as remote as y'all is up here."

Annette smiled. "I was talking about here. Just thinking out loud."

Buck walked out of the store and laid his bedroll across his horse's back and jammed his Winchester carbine firmly into the scabbard under the right side of his saddle. He unslung a canteen from his neck and draped the strap over his pommel, then slipped a big Remington revolver from his belt and dropped it into a leather pommel holster. He hummed loudly as he started to lash down his bedroll behind the saddle.

Junebug said, "You couldn't carry a tune in a bucket, Buck Watson. You got your slicker in that bedroll? It appears fat to me."

Buck grinned up at her. "Yes, I do, Boss Lady. You thunk I forgot it?"

"I thunk no such thing. I'm looking at them thunderheads off to the south, and I think you oughta pull that slicker out and just tie it on your saddle where you can get to it. Or toss it in the wagon, with mine and Bow Legs Annie's."

Buck stared at the black clouds for a second and said, "Good idea." He gave Annette a sheepish grin and added, "Don't know what I'd do without her, Miz Annette."

"Me neither," said Annette. "And I don't think you oughta try and find out. You see them extra boxes of cartridges I put on the counter in there for you?"

"Ahh, I seen 'em. Just didn't know they was for me. Us."

"And who in dickens else is fixing to ride off to God knows where, nearly 'bout alone today?" Annette tossed up her one remaining hand in exasperation and started inside. "Might'a been easier for you to have brung 'em, what with you having a full count of arms and hands and such. I'll go get 'em. And see can I get Bow Legs Annie's ample butt moving too."

"I'm right here, Miz Annette. And here's them bullets." Bow Legs Annie was a red-headed terror of a whore, one of the 'girls' who had come from the Gilded Lily brothel in Fort Worth with their madam Big Kate, two years ago. Annie tossed a large cloth satchel into the wagon, climbed up, then looked around expectantly. She broke into a broad grin and said, "And there you are your own self, Mister Hannity, you Black-Irish bugger."

Hannity, one of Count Baranov's two hired gunmen, walked up pulling his well-packed horse and carrying his trapdoor rifle. He smiled and tied his horse to a wagon wheel and said, "And a grand good morning to all. Faith, and it seems a fine time to ride off with friends on a wee adventure."

"Have you told the Count?" Annette asked. She had noticed Hannity spending more time with Bow Legs Annie of late and was hardly surprised at him leaving with her.

"And sure I have, Lady Balliett. He's not long for here himself, I'm thinking. He'll be off home across the ocean, once the good lady Janey Green moves on herself. Wasn't for him spending time with her, he'd likely already left us. Aye, and O'Reilly will get him to a train in Hays City, along of his precious Willi and pictures. Oh, and his new bones and skins and such, for his grand museum. O'Reilly has business back East, he does, as I do not, and the Count don't really need me no more."

Annette snorted. "Folks keep leaving or getting killed off, it's gonna turn right lonesome around here again." Once more she reached to scratch a nagging itch on her left forearm. Once more she was dejected to find it was still missing, the victim of a wrong-minded young buffalo hunter gone bad, now dead several years himself.

He'd been part of a gang that had torn through one night like a durn twister, bent on evil, while her son Dobey and his partner Boss Melton were off as Minutemen, chasing a band of Comanches. The gang had been white men, six of 'em, out of that Adobe Walls hunting camp upriver a piece. Their leader had raped and shot Dobey's wife Honey; left her half-dead and pregnant. Two others had raped and murdered Melton's wife Marie-Louise, while another had shot off Annette's arm and blown a hole through her blacksmith's chest. Old 'Nacio.

Annette stifled a sob as she turned toward the store. Ignacio had been more than a blacksmith; he'd been a lot more than a friend too, those last several years before he was killed, the years after her second husband had been murdered alongside 'Nacio's son.

"God, I miss 'em," she said as she trudged

toward the door. "Miss 'em all. Big Mac, little Becky, Timothy, young Tomaso, Marie-Louise, 'Nacio. Even more'n my durn arm." She paused as she realized she'd been speaking her thoughts, and turned back toward Junebug and the others, giving them a wry smile. "Only reason I don't leave here my own self, I reckon. Too much of my life is underground here."

CHAPTER SEVEN

Melton

"All right, Dobey, afore Doc and Buck come back from the creek, tell me just what the hell we're up to, busting our butts to get to Fort Richardson."

Dobey used his knife to turn the bacon slabs sizzling in the pan. "It's really Jacksboro, Jimmy, right there by Fort Richardson, but it's 'cause Buck said him and Junebug needs us. Hell, he near killed his horse getting to Canadian Fort in under five days."

"Hell, Dobey, I heard all that from Buck when he come in. Four ornery gunmen, a chickenshit lawman, I got all that. I meant what are we gonna do when we get there, what, maybe tomorrow?"

Dobey flipped some bacon on Melton's tin plate. "Yeah. Probably another sixty or seventy miles, so maybe late tomorrow. I figure we'll look up the lawman, see where the troublemakers are. Maybe they're sleeping one off and we can just go in fast and take 'em down without shooting. Knock 'em on the head, tie 'em up."

Melton grunted. "Your're always hopeful, ain't you? Even though you should know better. I say we just walk up to 'em and shoot 'em, afore they know what's up. Buck says they's randy as hell, prob'ly drunk and is known to have done some killing. You ain't going soft on me, is you, Cap'n?" Melton knew better, but liked to needle his young friend sometimes.

Dobey smiled. "Yeah, Jimmy, I thought we'd just ask 'em nice to just leave. Naw, it's just I want to know all I can before we move against 'em. It's still four against four, and Buck is kind of an unknown. He's fought some Indians but he sure ain't no hard-assed killer like you and Doc. Even if he was, it being even up, they could get lucky."

Melton said, "You're right again. I bet you get tired of that. Yeah. Was we to get young Buck shot up, Miss Junebug is likely to kill all of us. Who don't know that?"

Melton considered a bit before going on with his conversation with his partner and former commander. They'd ridden and fought together for over twelve years and thousands of miles, but that might count for nothing if Melton kept going down the trail of questions he was on the edge of. Didn't matter, he thought, I need to know, and might not be another time to ask.

"Dobey, they's something been eating at me for some time now. And I want to get it out in the open. That boy I hired as a horse-breaker, Mickey Ortega, right afore Tommy Christmas and Janey Green showed up. He was doing just fine, I thought, and you said so too, then he's gone. Like smoke in the wind. And all you ever said was, 'He left.' I know you run him off, but how come?"

Dobey turned as dark as a gathering storm. "You know I did? How do you know?"

Melton answered, "Big William let it slip but wouldn't say no more. And don't get snappy with me, neither." His voice rose. "We're supposed to be partners, and you ought to of talked it over with me. I kindly liked the boy and his work."

"Let it go, Jimmy." Dobey's voice was as dark as his face.

"Naw. I ain't letting it go, not no longer. I know you. You didn't cut him loose for no reason. If you'da caught him with Honey, you'da killed him. Did you catch him bothering Manuela? And if you did," his voice rose more, "how come you didn't just kill him?"

Dobey hesitated. Melton saw the fire leave him.

"Oh, shit," Melton said. "You did. And then you didn't want me to find out, did you. They was together, won't they." These weren't questions. "I knowed I was too old for her." Melton sagged.

Dobey said, "No. Sweet Jesus, no, Jimmy. Manuela doesn't look at anybody but you. Had nothing to do with her." He took a deep breath. "No. Listen. That time we were trailing those stampeded longhorns, and gave up on account of the rain. You remember?"

Melton nodded. He remembered it well. They'd come back by separate trails, still looking for the cattle, and Dobey had beat him home. When Melton got in several hours later, Mickey Ortega was gone.

Dobey went on. "Then you need to remember that all this happened while Honey was still messed up on laudanum and liquor, too. I walked in on her and Ortega. Thunder and all, they never heard me. I'd took off my muddy boots on the porch. She was lying on the bed, him standing over her, and she was touching him. Stroking him." Dobey's voice broke.

Melton said. "Did you kill him? He buried

somewhere nearby?"

Dobey said, "No. He froze when I cocked my pistol, but then I realized she was drunk. She was mumbling, 'Don't you like it, Dobey? Why don't you let me ever do this no more?' She thought he was me. He swore it never happened before. Said my mama sent him up to get her to come eat, and he'd just got there ahead of me. Said he pushed her hand away twice, and then I walked in. Said she kept calling him Dobey."

"Had his pants on?"

"Oh, hell, Jimmy, if he'd had one loose button he'da died right there. You know that. Naw, I just told him to ride. Said if I ever heard a whisper of such I'd hunt him down and kill him."

"You didn't even hit him none?"

"I might have swatted him once with the Remington. Maybe knocked loose a tooth. I mean, he coulda left sooner."

"Hell, Dobey, I'm sorry. What did she have to say?"

"Jimmy, I ain't ever even brought it up. Truth is, I don't like to think on it. I doubt she has any idea it ever happened. She got messed up on laudanum after she was shot and all, then she started buying liquor from hunters. Quit it all after Tommy Christmas showed up."

Melton said, "Yeah. And you started doing your job, and all. Listen. We all knew what was going on, so I told Doc not to let her have no more of that drug, and I got Junebug to give her some of that powder she used to get Doc to stop drinking. Look, I know that this was hard for you to let on, even to me. But I feel a whole lot better, and it's safe with me. As for Miguel Ortega, I'd of shot him. You let him off light. He shoulda run the minute Honey reached for him."

Buck
As they climbed back up the hill to the breakfast fire, Doc broke the uncomfortable silence.

"Buck, I need to hear that you're taking good care of my Junebug."

Buck paused. His heart had been in his throat ever since Doc said he'd walk down to the creek with him. Doc might have been a broke-down drunk of a dentist when they'd met in Masons Landing five years ago, but Junebug had been his working-girl sweetheart, and she'd got him sober along the way to Texas. Now Doc was a clear-eyed dentist and gambler. And killer. And Junebug was with Buck.

Buck threw up his hands, half-mad and

66

the other half-afraid, and spilled a good bit of the water from the coffee pot. "I am doing right by her, Doc. I told you I would. And she ain't yourn no more."

Doc froze him with those eyes. "I meant nothing rude. Nor did I mean to intrude, but I owe her a lot, and I care. I certainly did not mean to make your pour out our coffee water. Give me the damned pot and I'll go back and refill it. You go on and insure those two Cossacks save us some bacon. That mouthwatering aroma is enough to overwhelm me already."

Buck handed him the pot, and said "Yessir. I mean, thank you, Doc. I'll go right on up there, then." He pointed uphill, feeling deeply stupid.

Doc grunted. "And where else would you go?" He started back toward the creek. "Jesus, save me from the children."

Dobey

Buck squatted by the fire and said, "Doc'll be right along. He kind of made me spill the water, so he went back for more. Said don't y'all eat all the bacon. I see you ain't."

Dobey said, "Get your plate, unless you like scalded hands. And then tell me something. You ain't mentioned Hannity in all

67

this. Won't he be with us, making it five to four?"

Buck slapped his leg and said, "Aw shoot, Cap'n, I meant to tell you. Him and Bow Legs Annie didn't stay. Said she couldn't handle the trade by herself. Said they'd head on to Fort Worth, pick up a few more whores and be back soon as they could. Might be him and me coulda handled these boys if he was still up here."

Doc had walked up and heard the last exchange. He stuck the coffee pot down in the coals and said, "The long-shooter and you against four pistoleros? It's a good thing he did leave." Melton just snorted.

CHAPTER EIGHT

Dobey

"Jacksboro, Texas, ain't much of a town," Dobey said, mostly to himself. "And this ain't much of a courtroom."

Jimmy 'Boss' Melton just nodded.

Buck Watson said, "Yessir, Cap'n, but it'll do better now we got Fort Richardson here and all. And it's a whole lot closer to Fort Worth than Balliett's Post. Not so many Comanches and Kiowas and such."

Melton snorted. "We was in Hays City, Kansas, not more'n three months ago. It was like a big-assed city compared to this shit-hole. They both got a fort, but this is more like the end of the world."

Now Buck nodded nervously and Dobey thought, *Nobody wants to argue with Melton.*

The three unarmed men sat at a table in a ramshackle saloon, in front of the bar that held their two Yellowboy carbines and four Remington revolvers. A tall man stood behind the bar, his Dragoon Colt resting in front of him. The silver star on his hat marked him as a lawman. Even from six feet away, Dobey could read the words 'Texas Ranger' on his badge.

Dobey scanned the room. A few locals sat at tables behind him, and their sheriff stood talking to them. No one sat along the back wall, which was off to Dobey's right and by the back door. Back there, those four chairs still lay a-jumble in the pool of already black blood. To his left, Doctor Charles John Thomason leaned against the wall just inside the front door. Another pool of drying blood was there. The bodies had been carried out, and Dobey could hear the hammering from down the street where the five coffins were being knocked together.

Melton muttered, "Doc'll cover us till we get to our guns, do things go bad here."

Buck grinned. "Yessir. Ol' Chucky Jack has got our back. Hey, did you hear that? I made a kind of . . ."

Melton glared him back into silence, then muttered, "This ain't no time for no poetry."

The tall lawman banged the bar with his big revolver and said, "Let's get this over."

The town sheriff detached himself from the other group and strolled toward the bar. "I seen another Texas Ranger once. That

70

ain't the same badge he wore," he remarked, smirking back at his friends as he stopped by Dobey's chair.

Sweet Jesus, Dobey thought, do we smell as bad as him?

Melton looked up at the sheriff and said, "How 'bout you move your ass somewheres downwind?"

The Ranger motioned the sheriff to step closer. "They don't give us badges. We make 'em our ownselves, do we want one. You sent for a Ranger. Well, I'm Sergeant Cobb, 'F' Company, under Captain Baker. Tell me what happened here."

The sheriff cleared his throat. "Deets Hart and his two brothers and Chunk Tyler come to town, I dunno, maybe two weeks ago, started raising hell and all. Couple of days ago, ol' J.C. Clemmons throwed in with 'em, and they got worse, so I sent for you. These folks come into town today just before you got here. Two of 'em, them two there," he pointed toward Dobey and Melton, "they went in front here, carrying Winchesters. Little one there, the old bald one by the door, he stood out front and stopped me. Young one there at the table," the sheriff nodded at Buck, "he went around back. They was a bunch of shooting and yelling, then the big one come to the door and said,

71

'Y'all can come in now.' The old bald one, well, I didn't know he was bald then, had his hat on, see, but anyways he waved that fancy pistol at me and said, 'After you,' so I come on in." He stood there, nodding and smiling.

The Ranger shooed a fly from his nose and said, "And?"

"And what, your honor?"

"This ain't no dad blame court, and I ain't no durn judge, no more'n you're a real dadgum sheriff, you worthless little crawdad. What I am is busier than all heck. I'd like to finish this investigating afore next summer. Next half-hour would be way better. I ast you what happened here, as I got to decide whether to put this in front of the judge."

The big Ranger had piercing green eyes that wilted the shabby lawman. When two other locals snickered, those same eyes shifted to burn holes in them.

"Y'all want me to take the butt-end of this horse pistol to you, or you wanna just ease on out?" Sergeant Cobb jabbed a finger at the door, and the two culprits muttered apologies and crept outside. The Ranger turned back to the sheriff and raised his eyebrows.

The sheriff took off his hat and twisted it

in front of him. "Oh, well, that's about it. It was over. Chunk Tyler, he was on his back over there, 'tween the bar and the front door. Hat over his face, shotgun across his legs. Lots of blood. Lung shot, I'd say. These two what come in the front, they was standing there in the middle still holding them carbines. And the young one must of come in the back door, he was over to the back end of the bar, reloading his pistols. Them two cut-down Remingtons there." He licked his lips, then continued. "Deets Hart and both his brothers and J.C. Clemmons was all laying against the back wall, all four of 'em dead, all mixed in with them turned-over chairs. Shot all to hell."

"So you heard shooting but didn't see nothing." The Ranger rubbed his temples, then squinted at the squirming lawman again. "You got any dadgum witnesses?"

Dobey started to speak, but Melton beat him to it. "All three of us," he grinned.

Sergeant Cobb said, "I mean aside from you three, dadblast it. Y'all is the accused here. I'll hear you out, but lastmost. So's you can kind of like push back against whatever is said against you, and all. Jehosaphat."

The sergeant looked around the room. "If don't nobody else step up, these three can

73

say they was sipping sasparilly at the bar while those five shot each other."

"I seen most of it, Sergeant." The speaker was a slender woman, almost pretty but hard-faced. She had pushed past a drape from a side room and put a steaming cup in front of the startled Ranger. "You look like you could use some coffee."

The Ranger stared at her. "Well, thankee, I surely could, but who in tarnation are you?"

"Junebug. This here's my place. Mine and Buck's, that is." She nodded toward Buck. "Buck Watson there is my man, and I sent him to Balliett's Post 'bout ten days ago to get these other men. We use to live there. I knew they'd help us."

"Balliett's Post. Up on the South Canadian river, ain't it? And why'd you need their help, from two hundred fifty miles away?"

"Well, we don't know nobody else, and them good ol' boys had been terrorizing the whole town, what little there is of it, for most of a week. Just taking whatsoever they wished, women, food, liquor, cigars, you name it, they took it. Never paid for nothing neither, and then picked on farmers come to town. Hollering, cussing, taking the Lord's name in vain — and I won't

74

stand for that."

Dobey and the other accused men nodded in agreement, and the bald one by the door said, "God's truth."

The Ranger said, "I don't care for that none myself." He patted Junebug's arm and said, "Go right on."

"Only reason they didn't do more harm is I got 'em knee-crawling drunk several days at a time. I could see our no-count sheriff wasn't doing nothing. Then this morning the sheriff told 'em that he had sent for the Rangers. They laughed at him, but when we got word only one Ranger was coming, they run the sheriff off and set up here to ambush you. That Chunk Tyler took me back in the kitchen, held a shotgun on me. Other four was against the back wall. Chunk was gonna shotgun you from behind when you come in."

"But your friends got here first."

"Yessir. And when Chunk let go of me and stepped out behind 'em, I throwed hot coffee on him, just as Buck busted in from the back and shot him. And then Buck shot the other four. And then Boss Melton let the Sheriff and Doc in. And then you showed up."

"Hold on. Hold on just a goldurn minute here. You say that boy shot all five of 'em?"

"Yessir. Yes he did. And he ain't no boy, neither. If I'd knowed he was that good, I wouldn'ta even sent for no help." The pride beamed right off her face.

"Good God Almighty!" The Ranger stared at Buck, who blushed like a young girl.

Junebug raised a finger to the Ranger and said, "You watch your mouth."

The Ranger held up both hands in surrender, grinned for the first time, and said, "Yessum. Sorry." Turning to the sheriff, he said, "You real sure you wanna push charges on this?"

The sheriff whined, "Well, I wouldn't of said nothing to start with, 'cept they put me down pretty bad before you got here, in front of ever'body. Said I didn't do my job and all. Called me a coward . . ."

The Ranger dismissed him. "This is over. The killings was justified. Y'all put your guns back on, but don't go shooting this so-called lawman while I'm still in town."

CHAPTER NINE

Dobey

Dobey took a sip of whiskey, grimaced and said, "So Buck, what're y'all calling this fine establishment?"

Dobey and Buck were sharing drinks at a table with Jimmy Melton and Doc Thomason, in the very room where five men had died two hours earlier. The floor under them was heavily coated with sand to cover and absorb the blood. The picket walls, chinked with mud and pebbles, kept a lot of the wind out.

"I said just call it Junebug's Place, but she wants something fancier. 'Buckeroo Club' was what she come up with," Buck grinned. "Likes it 'cause of my name being in it, and all. It's what folks call them wild-ass young cowboys coming through here."

Doc snorted. "Buckaroo. It's from *vaquero,* the Mexican word for a horseman who works cattle. But enough of this chil-

77

dren's chatter. I want to know what really happened in here. I find it difficult to believe that you two Cossacks stood idly by while this boy killed five armed men."

Melton said, "It's for real, Doc. Dobey and I come in fast, caught four of 'em sitting against this back wall. Had 'em covered. All of a sudden that door there pops open and here comes Mister Buck, a cut-down Remington in each hand, throws one up and puts a shot right by my left side. Thought he was shooting at me for a second. Heard noise behind me, I turn and there's that Chunk feller slammed against the wall and sliding down, and Miss Junebug standing by the curtain holding a pot. I turned back, and there's Buck blazing away down the wall at the other four as they's trying to get up out'n their chairs. Sort of had 'em in a line, and was letting fly with both pistols. It was over before I could fire a shot."

Dobey looked at Melton for a second, then nodded. "Me neither, nor any of them. Seems like somebody was yelling all through it, but I don't know who, or maybe I just heard it in my head. But that's the way it went down, Doc."

Doc shook his head. "I heard the yelling too, outside and above the gunfire. I suppose it was those men dying."

Junebug walked up and heard the last part. She refilled Doc's coffee. "I think it might have been me screaming," she said.

Melton said, "It was more like the old Rebel Yell."

Buck whispered, "It was me. Y'all don't need to tell nobody, all right? I don't know what come over me. When I went around back I thought we was only going up against the three Hart brothers and Chunk Tyler, but they was five horses back there. I was trying to yell a warning as I run in, but all that come out was the yell. Y'all please tell me I didn't sound like no girl."

"Well," said Melton, "I ain't about to say no such thing. Ain't likely that anybody else will, neither. You was in a blood rage. I think if you hadn't of run dry in both pistols, you might'a charged back outside, yelled at their horses and shot them too."

Dobey said, "I never seen the likes of it."

"Nor have I," said Doc, "but I have heard of something very similar. It was Melton's comment that reminded me. During the war, a wounded captain of infantry passed through Mason's Landing, going home. He'd lost one eye and had a mangled leg. He told me his company had been sent to flank a Yankee artillery piece in some woods. To insure surprise he had his men de-cap their rifles and fix bayonets. They could hear the cannon banging away, of course, and when they got close they saw there was no infantry protecting the gun crew. Just then the crew chief yelled out to load grapeshot. The captain said he started screaming 'No,' and charged out of the bushes, firing his pistol. He forgot to order his men to re-cap their rifles, but they followed him, screaming too. They bayoneted all of the artillerymen. Every one of them." Doc paused for a deep breath. "There were only six or seven Yankees, and he still had twenty men left in his company."

"My God," said Buck.

"That isn't all. They kept going and bayoneted the artillery horses, too. Six of them in limber harness to pull the gun, four more for the little ammunition wagon, and several others tethered separately, for the officer and sergeants, I suppose. Innocent as children. He said the horses screamed louder than his men."

There was dead silence, as the hard men listening to the doctor struggled to absorb that horrible vision.

Doc continued. "I am sure they hated enemy artillery. Grapeshot, canister, killing from a distance, riding instead of walking, better food, all that. Surely, though, they didn't hate horses. I think it must have been pent-up fear and rage that could only have been slaked by much blood and yelling. But I can only imagine."

Dobey said, "How was he with that? Killing the horses, I mean."

"Near insane, I think," said Doc. "He and his men had made a pact to tell no one, ever, as they were ashamed and didn't understand their own actions. He only told me after a large amount of rye whiskey."

Melton muttered, "Jesus."

Doc stared into the distance, right through the wall of the saloon. "I think he was better the next day, having talked about it. And having received no condemnation from me for actions he couldn't explain. That was seven years ago. Still, he might well have drunk himself to death by now, except . . ." He stopped and shook his head.

"Except what, Doc?"

Doc coughed. "The next day, one of those despicable deputies was abusing a horse, and the captain attacked him, beating him with his crutch. That scoundrel Marshal Fetterman shot the cripple dead."

Melton scowled and thumped the table with the heel of his fist. "We shoulda killed Fetterman when we had him. I told you so at the time, Dobey. I know it woulda been too late for the cripple, but at least Fetter-man wouldn'ta got away with it. He should burn in Hell."

Buck said, "After what he did to us, he ought to burn right here on earth."

It was quiet for a bit, except for the wind whistling through cracks in the walls, and a piece of tin roof flapping somewhere nearby.

Doc stood and said, "If that damned wind ever lets up, everyone will have to learn to walk upright again. I'm going for more coffee." He pushed through the drape into the kitchen.

Melton turned to Buck and said, "So, I got a bone to pick with you. You told me once, way back when we first seen you with a Winchester carbine, that the rifle version would hold seventeen rounds in the magazine. I borrowed Bear's rifle a while back and couldn't get but fifteen in his. Took it back to the store we bought it from, raised hell with the owner, come to find out ain't none of 'em hold but fifteen. Made a total damn fool of myself. It's a good thing you wasn't there after I apologized to that feller. Now, tell me about these cut-down Remingtons of yours. What did you take, three inches off'n the barrels?"

"Three, maybe three and a half, Boss.

They's a Mex gunsmith here. You apologized?"

Doc

In the kitchen, Doc stared hard at Junebug as she refilled his cup. "That boy out there. Is he treating you well? No regrets about moving here yet?"

She met his gaze. "He ain't no boy, Doc. He does look out for me, and he works like a dog. So, no, I ain't sorry, 'cept for missing ever'body back in Canadian Fort."

"If you miss us, why did you leave? I was no threat to young Mister Buck."

"The hell you weren't, Doc. He's always gonna worry is he as good as you. In all kinds of ways." Junebug shrugged. "Least-ways here, you ain't around all the time to play on his mind. Big thing, though, is I wanted my own saloon and whorehouse. Weren't no room for another, alongside of you and Melton's sister. And they is a mess of soldiers here, when they ain't out chasing Comanches and Kioways."

Doc drained his coffee and set the cup in the wash pan. "Well, you should know you're missed. And not just you. And not just by me."

Junebug touched his arm. "Thank you, Doc. Thanks for telling me. Now you got to

83

go back out there and try and say that to Buck, 'cause right now he's sitting out there about to mess his pants, wondering what's going on in here."

Doc squeezed her arm gently then pushed through the door curtain back into the bar, just as the Ranger returned through the front door.

"Whoo-Dawg," said the Ranger. "Getting a mite chilly out there." He dropped his hat on an empty table, sat with the others and began knuckling his eyes. "I swear, I got enough dust in my eyes and nose and ears to need a plow. Here's the thing, folks. I couldn't find no paper on none of them dead men, so's there ain't no reward. Good news is that so-called sheriff cut out south soon as he walked out of here. Town owed him some pay, so that'll take care of the burying of them five unfortunates. The other thing is that the town leaders was all aflutter about us running off their local lawman. I told 'em they had a real fine replacement right here in Buck Watson, if they paid you right. And if you don't want to be sheriff, I'll hire you in a skinny minute as a Texas Ranger."

Junebug placed a full coffee mug in front of Sergeant Cobb. "Oh, he'll take that sheriff's job. I mean, won't you, Buck,

Honey?"

Doc grinned and said, "I don't doubt he will," then looked at Melton and said, "Well, Cossack, why don't we take the new sheriff and ride out to that fort and introduce the leadership to the new law here? Make certain they know what happened here today? Might save the lives of a few Blue-coats."

Melton tossed off his whiskey and grinned. "Not a bad idea. Leastways, not for a scrawny, bald headed old tooth doc-tor. Then can we head home?"

Dobey wasn't grinning. "Yeah. And maybe we can find something out about Red and Penn's whereabouts."

Outside, the Ranger sergeant pulled Doc, Dobey, and Melton aside. "I got to head back to camp now, but I'll look in on your friend Buck ever' now and then. One thing though. Y'all didn't fool me none, saying y'all didn't shoot. I picked up two fired Henry shell casings off'n the floor in there when I looked the place over. Still warm. I don't appreciate being lied to, but I could see why you didn't speak up. You want that boy to be feared as someone who killed five gunmen by hisself. Ain't no question but that'll help him here."

Melton said, "It won't something we

planned. Hell, we didn't even talk about first. It just come to me as you was talking, and Dobey kind of followed my lead."

Dobey said, "Far as I know, Buck did kill 'em all. Could be both of us shot dead men. But does it make any difference?"

"Naw," said the Ranger. "Nary bit. The secret is safe with me."

"It's a good secret," said Doc. "But I knew these two didn't merely watch, not standing ready and wired tight, with cocked Winchesters."

"Say what?"

Doc grinned. "These two, in that situation and not shoot? Maybe if they were mere children again. Otherwise it was preordained gunfire."

■ ■ ■ ■ ■

1871

■ ■ ■ ■

CHAPTER TEN

Buck

"You ain't about to make no trouble for us now, is you, mistuh lawman? 'Cause we ain't done nobody wrong, and we ain't drinking or nothing."

Buck stared at the stocky Negro standing by his wagon on the main road through Jacksboro. The man wore a Remington conversion in a belt holster, his left hand resting on the butt. His right hand was close to a Yellowboy carbine in the driver's box. Buck wondered why he was so testy. Another Negro sat in the second large wagon, humming loudly and staring off into space. He quit humming, glanced at Buck and said, "Come on, Boss. Don't be starting nothing. Let's just roll. He's that killer." He began to hum again, but louder. Buck realized the second man wasn't talking to him.

Buck said carefully, "How come y'all think I'd make trouble for you?"

The first man said, "You see a nigger, got some guns, two wagons, got a nigger helper, you think right off, ain't no way he a bidness man. He trouble. Got to straighten him out. Well, that ain't right. I ain't done nothing wrong."

Buck saw that the man was really nervous. "I ain't said you did. Hell, I ain't said much of nothing, afore you got your back up. I just come over to ask where y'all was heading."

"We just come from Weatherford and headin' back west, down the Butterfield Road. Why? We ain't bothering no one."

"Never said you was," said Buck. "But the Rangers say there's some Comanches or Kiowas running about, and maybe y'all oughta hook up with some other folks or a patrol or something, other than making that run alone. Let's start over. I'm Sheriff Buck Watson. I ain't got nothing against darkies with guns. Nor anybody else, neither, if they ain't shooting up my town." He stuck his hand out.

"Britton Johnson," said the other man. He pulled off a tattered work glove and shook Buck's hand. Carefully. "Mostly folks call me Nigger Britt. Go figure on that." He finally smiled. Almost.

"I've heard of you," Buck said. "Business

90

man. Run some wagons between Weatherford and Fort Griffin. Freed afore the war
was over, and get on pretty good with the
Indians. Right?"

"Sort of. And we heard of you. Kilt like
twelve men with twelve shots, right over
there in the Buckaroo Club?"

Buck grinned. "It was in the old building,
not that new one there. And it was only five
men, and ten shots. And I'm pretty certain
two friends was shooting too. Story gets better ever' time I hear it."

Johnson stared at Buck for a second, then
said, "Lord. You's serious, ain't you? You
kilt five men, and you don't think that's
enough to make a nigger nervous?"

They were interrupted by the approach of
a third wagon driven by another Negro. The
wagon was led by a lanky rider wearing the
lone star of a Ranger.

"Sergeant Cobb," said Buck.

Cobb nodded. "Sheriff. Nigger Britt. Y'all
have met?" He ignored the other Negro
driver.

Buck said, "Just now."

Johnson said, "Yassir, Ranger Cobb." Buck
noticed the change in Britt Johnson's tone.
Respect was not the same sound as fear. It
was better.

Sergeant Cobb leaned on his pommel.

91

"Your man says y'all is going on to Fort Griffin today, Nigger Britt."

The other driver quit humming again and started singing some old hymn.

"We is," said Johnson. "Been gone already, 'cept this one had to visit his woman."

"I can't tell you different," said Cobb, "but I can say I don't advise it. Kioway has come down across the Red River agin, running wild. Matter of fact, I come in to tell Sheriff Buck Watson here we might need him to bring his Winchester and ride with us Rangers. Soon."

Britt Johnson said, "Nossir, bidness won't wait. I been dealing with The Folk for years, and we needs to get on to Fort Griffin. Did we worry and hide ever' time they's Kioway or Comanche about we'd have no life at all. Or bidness." He stepped on the wheel hub and swung into the driver's box. Two clucks and a snap of the reins and the mules began pulling the three wagons away.

The Buckaroo Club was in a much better building than where it began. The two-story place wasn't packed but there was a good-sized crowd, a mixture of Bluecoats, drovers, gamblers, and working girls. Buck and Sergeant Cobb shared a table in a corner away from the bar, and Hannity joined them. Junebug brought them drinks, then moved to calm down a drunk soldier.

It was early afternoon, not long after Britt Johnson's wagons had left. It was also January and bitter cold. Sergeant Cobb said he could have one drink against the weather before he rode back to camp. Buck figured him for two.

The Ranger slugged down his drink and signaled for another. "Durn. I just hope my pizzle stick don't freeze and break off in that wind out there. I feel plumb brittle all over." He nodded thanks as his second drink arrived then said, "You know Nigger Britt's story?"

"Sure, and one hears things, but who can you trust? A Ranger, now, there's the word of a man for me," said Hannity.

Buck just nodded, then signaled the bartender for coffee.

Cobb began. "His family was half killed and half captured by Kioway in '64 whilst he was off doing something for his owner. His owner died 'bout then, sort of setting him free, so's he spent the next many months pushing up into the Territory, time and agin, trying to recover his family. He got some of 'em back in '65. They's a question if his woman wanted to come home."

Hannity just stared at the Ranger. Buck

said, "Now, come on."

"Naw," said Cobb. "it's true. Was another case like it, a ways back. A girl name of Cynthia Ann Parker was took when she was maybe nine back in the '30's. She later on married into the Comanches, had babies and all, then Rangers retook her and a daughter 'bout ten years ago. She'd been with the Comanches near twenty-five years."

Buck said, "You're putting us on."

"Nope," Cobb said. "She tried to go back to the tribe ever' time she could get loose, but the good white people of Texas wouldn't let her. You know how gov'mint knows best. The daughter caught fever and passed, then Cynthia Ann died 'bout a year ago. One of her other kids is a Comanche chief, so I hear. Quantum or Kuanai, or some Injin name like that."

Hannity said, "What has that to do with the Negro Johnson?"

"Nary a thing," said Cobb. "Anyhow, Nigger Britt ain't just a business man, he's pretty durn fearless. Goes among them heathens with just a pistol and a Yellowboy carbine. Probably live forever."

"I think we're about done for the night, Buck. You ready to head upstairs?" Junebug was wiping off tables in the bar as she spoke. "They's still two men up there with the girls, but they said they was laying over for breakfast."

Buck stood at the bar, sipping coffee. "You go ahead up," he said. "I need to make one more swing through town, afore putting my head down."

Hannity, behind the bar, dried the last two glasses and said, "Want company on that cold trip?"

Buck almost declined; he felt guilty about asking Hannity to join him in the late January weather. "Normal, I'd say no. As it is, I do wanna talk to you 'bout something. It ain't no way important, though. Tomorrow'd be fine, if'n you're tired."

"God love you, lad. But," Hannity paused to down a shot of whiskey, "there's nothing like warm whiskey, a cold walk, and unimportant talk to make a bed comfortable. Lemme grab me coat and the shotgun."

Outside, the wind hit them hard. "Freezing or below, I'd say," said Buck, as he tied his kerchief over his hat and ears.

"Sure, and it's a measure of how scared I am to refuse a request from you." Hannity grinned as he pulled his collar up. "Else and no way I'd be out here, my pecker froze hard but small."

"You joke on it, but that's what I wanted

to talk to you about. You heard Ranger Cobb say that darky Britt Johnson was fearless, right?"

Hannity nodded.

Buck continued, "Well, when I come up to him the other day, he was afraid. I mean, not just nervous about me being white and the law, but scared. And he won't scared of Ranger Cobb."

Hannity stopped and stared at him. "You serious? You don't know?"

Buck shrugged. "Johnson asked me the same thing. Then he said it was that shootout we was in . . ."

"YOU was in. Not 'we.' That was all you, and that's why folks is scared of you. Faith, now, ain't nobody seen anything like it. Everybody is scared of you. 'Cept me, of course. And Dobey, Doc and Boss Melton. And Ranger Cobb. And, truth be known, all of us should be, too. Jaysus, lad, five dead men in under five seconds? Jaysus!"

"But I ain't changed none. Not none at all."

"Not to you, maybe," said Hannity. "But to ever'body else? Listen, it ain't a bad thing. I'm supposed to be the bouncer, but all's I have to do is say to trouble makers, 'D'ye know this place is Sheriff Buck Watson's?' They piss down their legs and

96

start apologizing and buying me drinks. Faith, and I love it."

They were interrupted by the slowing thud of hooves and the clank and jingle of two wagons rolling in from the west.

"And it's after two of the morning," said Hannity. "What's this now?"

Buck stepped into the street and stopped the wagons, which contained four frightened men.

"Injuns," their leader said. "We drove all afternoon and all night. Three burned wagons, six dead mules, and three dead schwartzers burned or cut all to pieces, back along this Butterfield Road. We been scared shitless. Jah, for sure."

"Ah," said Hannity. "Sounds like the fearless Negro Britt Johnson. Not good."

Fifteen minutes later, the exhausted freighters were wolfing down warmed-up soup, coffee, and bread in the Buckaroo Club; Buck stood at the bar with Hannity and Junebug.

"I s'pose we better start waking ever'body up," said Buck. "We don't know how many Injins they was, nor if they'll come here next."

"You do no such of a thing," said Junebug. "You'll cause a panic. Folks'll be shooting

97

harmless Tonkaways and each other, like as not. Them Comanches or Kioways or whatever they is, they ain't coming here, not with the fort so near."

Buck frowned. "Well, I can't just do nothing, neither."

Junebug turned soothing. "No, Buck, honey, I know you can't. Mustn't. Which of them muleskinners is the boss?"

Hannity said, "The fat German there. Otto Something-or-other."

"Buck, you take him, put him on Hannity's horse and take him out to the fort. Tell 'em we don't want to rouse folks up. See will they send out a patrol. Come morning, we can tell the townfolk and say the army's on top of it. What do you think?"

What Buck thought was that she was the smart one, and it was right kindly of her to ask. He nodded slowly then said, "That's good thinking, Boss Lady. Hannity, I still think you should go and wake up three or four steady men, maybe Caddo James, Greg Banks, couple more like that, and put 'em out at the town corners. Leastways 'til dawn."

Now Hannity nodded. "And I will, Buck. On horseback."

Junebug patted Buck's arm. "That's a smart move, honey. Just in case."

■ ■ ■ ■

The twenty troopers from the Sixth Cavalry made good time through the rest of that long January night and most of the next day. Buck rode with the grizzled sergeant commanding the section, several hundred yards behind the two Tonkawa scouts.

Buck said, "How come the commander didn't send no officer? He thinks pretty high of you?"

The sergeant shrugged. "We known each other a long time. And he knows I was a colonel in the Alabama cavalry. And we ain't got but one lieutenant who knows his own ass from first base, and he's my company commander."

Buck said, "First base?"

"It's part of a ball game we been playing for a while now. Whoa — looks like something's up now. Here comes one of the Tonks."

One of the scouts dropped back beside them and said, "Close now. Them trees up ahead. See the birds?"

Now Buck noticed the circling buzzards and was ashamed he hadn't registered them already.

"Wide awake now, boys. Unshuck them

carbines." The sergeant pulled his own Spencer, made sure it was on half-cock, then levered the breech open a half-inch to check for a round in the chamber.

Buck did the same thing with his Winchester. So did the twenty troopers, without being told.

"They is well trained," said the sergeant. "The cheese do get a little more binding now, but I don't worry none. These boys is tough, and most of 'em been in a fight or two. I got twenty-one seven-shot Spencers, same number of revolvers, and the killingest sheriff in Texas. We can take on eighty Comanches if need be, though I 'spect they's long gone."

The smell of death almost choked Buck as they rode past the Tonks onto the slaughter grounds. One of the Tonks said, "Not Nermernuh. Kiowa, yes."

"That's mainly them mules you smell. Some Injins don't care none for 'em." The sergeant pulled a frayed cloth kerchief up over his nose. "Why don't you bang off a couple shots with one of them cah'tridge pistols of yourn, scare off them buzzards? My Remington is cap and ball. Slower to reload."

Buck noticed the wolves had already pulled away to a low ridge, a hundred yards north. He fired two shots in their direction, kicking up dirt and pushing them back another fifty yards. The buzzards all flapped away to gain altitude. And wait.

"Snell, take your half section and put 'em out some in all directions, maybe a hunnert yards. Make sure you got somebody on the far side of them trees and that little ridge. Mason, your boys start digging. We need one big grave. I'll rotate Snell's boys in to finish up in a hour or two. I want to be away from this damn smell afore dark. Sheriff, let's us look this mess over."

They rode in a slow circle around the killing field. The three wagons were maybe thirty or forty yards off the stage trail. They were all a jumble of burned wood and metal. On the driver's seat of the one nearest the trees sat a charred body, lips pulled back in a hideous grin, the stubs of a dozen burnt arrows sticking out of his body. And legs. And head.

"Jesus," muttered Buck. "He must have been pinned to that seat with arrows."

"Yep, I'd say so. And him and the wagons was doused with coal oil, so's they'd burn. Him still burning as they left is prob'ly why he ain't cut up more. Lookit that nigger over towards the trees."

The second body was half way from the

trees to the wagons, on his back. He might have been staring at the sky, but his eyes were gone. So were his eye lids, and hair, and privates. He was cut open from neck to groin, and his entrails were strung away into the grass. His pants were around his knees and they were soiled with more than blood.

"Jesus," Buck said again. "He shit his pants."

"Prob'ly why The Folk didn't take 'em. I 'spect they caught him doing his business in them trees, and chased him here, playing with him."

The dead man had at least ten arrows in him, and both thighs were sliced to the bone.

"At least they didn't cut out his tongue," said Buck.

"That ain't his tongue, Sheriff. That's his pecker. Little frontier humor, courtesy of The Folk."

"Why you call 'em that? The Folk, I mean."

"It's what the Kioway call themselves. The Folk. The People. Their partners now, some calls 'em Comanch or Comanches, but they call themselves Nermernuh. The True Humans. I calls 'em all murdering thieving bastards." The sergeant spat, then cut two chunks from a plug of tobacco. "Have a chaw, Sheriff. It'll help with the smell. And the bile."

The third body was inside a small fort made with dead mules. It was as bad as the second body but was naked. They dismounted.

"This un's Nigger Britt," said the sergeant, squatting. "I'd know from his size even if'n he weren't surrounded by empty Henry cah'tridges." He turned the man's head from side to side, then stood. "Britt carried a conversion Remington, like yourn. Didn't blow no hole in his head, so The Folk must've tooken him alive. That weren't good."

Later, after Johnson's body had been dragged off to the common grave, Buck counted 72 empty shell casings in his 'fort,' and the Tonks showed him more than a dozen bloody patches where Kiowas had suffered.

They headed back east shortly before dark. Buck looked back at the patch of prairie and said, "That was a real battlefield, won't it?"

"Yep," said the sergeant, pulling down his kerchief to suck in the cold air. "He must of held 'em off a couple of hours. Hurt 'em bad so they hurt him bad when they final tooken him. And a few year go by, won't nobody know what happened here."

When they finally returned to Jacksboro late the next day, Buck was slow to tell Junebug what he'd seen. They stood at the bar sipping coffee.

"You ain't getting no food nor anything else might interest you 'til I hear the whole thing, Buck Watson. Give it up."

He started slow, but it was like a dam breaking. It all poured out. The outrage, the smell, the destruction, even the fear on the ride home. Then he told her what the old sergeant said about nobody remembering it.

She put her hands on her hips. "Well, that just ain't right. It don't matter that he were a darky, nor even some slant eyed Chinee washerman. Somebody puts up a stand like that, he needs to be recalled. Ought to be a marker or something."

Buck said, "You know that ain't gonna happen. Not for no darky. Not out here."

"That don't make it right," she snapped. "We got to tell ever'body we can. Don't let no one forget. Not never." She stomped her foot and spun to walk away.

The foot-stomping caused Buck to jump a little and he was going to agree with her but before he could even mumble his usual

"Yes, Honey," she turned back to him and started again.

"And another thing. You get a wagon and Hannity or somebody, maybe that Sergeant Cobb, and y'all go to Weatherford and tell his woman what happened to him, as much as you can. Maybe not as much as you tole me, but then see can you bring her and whatever kids she has left and bring 'em here."

"Here? But, what if she don't want to, uh . . ."

"I ain't talking about making her no whore. She can if she wants, and welcome. All's I mean is to get her work, here or to the fort. Sewing, laundry, cooking, whatever. It's a hardscrabble life out here for any woman, just to scratch by. Think what she's looking at as a widow darky. With a child. Maybe two." She snuffled. "Makes me sad to think on it. Why'd you start me on it, anyways?" She snatched a wiping cloth from the bar, dabbed her eyes then blew her nose in it.

"You crying, Junebug? I ain't ever seen you . . ."

"Nor you ain't now, neither. Durn drover opened that door and I got sand in my eye is all. I'll get you some food. You can go to Weatherford in the morning."

CHAPTER ELEVEN

Honey

The adobe fort that was the main building of Balliett's Trading Post faced north, toward the river and Hogtown on the other side. Most traffic came from that direction, so the massive wooden gate was on that side, and the gate was the only feature which gave the mud fortress a face.

Otherwise, it was oblong with fighting towers jutting out of the northwest and southeast corners. It was nearly two-hundred feet long ways, by ninety feet across. Dobey had designed it. His brother Tad had supervised the construction, which was performed by everyone else who lived there, including the children.

"And not a few innocent bystanders," Doc had commented, referring to the hunters, Mexican traders, soldiers, and other hungry passers-by who'd been "encouraged" to work for their otherwise free food.

"Our Big-Assed Soddy," is what Melton called it. A few cats took care of rodents and tarantulas, and one dog had become expert at sniffing out rattlers and scorpions and sounding a peculiar yipping alarm. A couple of fast horses were brought inside at night in case the remuda was taken in a raid and help needed to be sent for.

The fighting towers provided enfilading fire down all four walls, which so far hadn't been needed. The towers also provided a couple of sort of private chambers for "married" couples inside the fort, who could "volunteer" for tower duty with the understanding that, if the trap door at the top of the stairs was closed, then the couple wouldn't be disturbed. The couples all had sleeping quarters on the ground floor of course, but those were shared with children. Normal children. Nosy.

Since the towers were designated as "last stand" positions, those trap doors could also be securely bolted from inside against attacking hostiles. Or nosy children. There were buffalo robes and an adobe oven in one inside corner, and jerky and firewood and water. And a basin and some washcloths, for freshening up.

Because Dobey was riding north in the morning, Honey had pulled rank to take an early shift in the northwest tower. She wanted to finish their lovemaking in time to let Dobey get some sleep.

A violent storm was west and north of them, moving slowly east. "I guess we'll ride through that tomorrow," Dobey muttered, as he pulled off his boots. He grinned at Honey. "Leastways, all that thunder will maybe cover some of your screaming and hollering."

Honey pulled off her shirt and tossed it on top of her dress, then snuggled against him and began stroking his hard stomach.

"I thought you like me getting all excited and noisy," she murmured, nibbling at his nipple. "Besides, it's your doing."

"You know I like it," he said, "Just worry sometimes that folks might think I'm murdering you."

"You ought to worry you *might* kill me one night, putting your durn hand over my mouth to quiet me."

Later, as they lay gasping for breath, her on top, she buried her face in his chest hairs. "You can take your hand off my mouth now, Thomas. You maybe noticed I finished?"

"Don't nobody call me that but you and Mama," he wheezed. "Good Lord. You still take my breath completely away. And I didn't put my hand on your mouth this time. I was just stroking your face."

She raised her head to stare into his eyes. "I noticed that. Thank the Lord for thunder, huh?"

He exhaled. "Yes, ma'am. And for you."

She folded her hands on his chest, like she was praying, and rested her chin on them. "Thomas, ain't no way how I can ever explain how happy I've been since you found your way back to me. I'm gonna miss you . . ."

He said, "Honey, I —"

She put a finger on his lips and said, "Shut up, now, and listen to me. I'm gonna miss you, but I want you to get this and take it with you. I want you to go. I want you to go and find that black-hearted man Red, and kill him for what he put you through. And Penn, for what he did to my mama. You need to know that's how I feel. It's how I can tolerate you being gone so much."

"You always say that, like I was the main one hurt. Not you."

"No man ought to go through that. Knowing another man took his woman by force." Thomas' mother had taught her to say that. "I hate him for that more than what he done to me. And if I didn't have these children to care for, I'd go after him my ownself. I

109

could kill him, Thomas. You know that." Tears spilled down her face.

He pulled her head down on his chest and stroked her tangled black hair.

"I know you could," he said. "Hell, you tried. You shot him. Easy, now."

She pulled her head up to stare at him again, eyes glistening but blazing now. "Yes I did, and I'm sorry I failed to kill him, else you wouldn't be still going through this. You find him and kill him, but more'n that, you come back. You promise me. I need you, and these children need you. Our'n, and your'n and mine."

"You listen to me now. They're all three ours. Ain't none of 'em nobody else's."

"You're right, Thomas. They are gifts from Heaven."

She sat up and reached for a washcloth. "Let's go tuck 'em in."

"All right, Boss Lady. And let someone else use this boudoir, right?"

She wiped away a tear, then squeezed ice cold water on his naked crotch. He jumped up and said, "Guess I won't use that again tonight. You plumb shriveled me."

She said, "You'd best not even think about using it thataway for the next few weeks, at least. If you want to keep it, that is."

She cleaned up and dressed quickly, as

Dobey struggled with his boots. Sliding the lock-bolt aside, she lifted the heavy door — to find six year old Tommy Christmas asleep on the ladder. He was seated on the third rung, legs dangling free, with his head down on both arms folded on the top rung.

"Lord, Thomas, lookit this," she whispered. "Don't say nothing, mon cheri, he could fall. Get his arms."

Dobey squatted, put his thumbs in the boy's armpits, and lifted him straight up. Honey knelt and untangled Tommy's legs as her husband pulled him to safety.

"You think he heard much?"

"I think he heard a bunch of thunder, Honey, and come looking for us. He's out cold." Dobey hugged the boy to his chest as he studied those steps. "No way I can carry him down, though, and he can't sleep here. Tommy. Tommy! Wake up, son."

Tommy rubbed his eyes and looked around, then hugged Dobey's neck. "Don't go, Daddy."

"I got to, Tommy. I told you. Got to get your Aunt Janey to the train."

"Then let me go too, Daddy. I can shoot. You taught me good."

"I know you can shoot, boy. That's why I need you to stay here and keep lookout for Mama."

"She ain't my real mama," he snuffled. "My real mama's in heaven."

Dobey held him straight out. "Listen to me, boy . . ."

Honey took Tommy from him and said, "You ease on down, Thomas, and I'll hand him down. Now, Tommy, I need you to help me. See, my real mama died and went to heaven 'bout the same time yours did. Did you know that? Well, it's true. Since then your daddy's mama has become my second mama. God gave her to me, just like he sent you to me to help with my hurt. I think God wants me to be your second mama, like Mama Balliett is mine. It would make me real happy if you'd let me do that."

"You mama is up with my mama?"

"Yes, she is. They're up there watching us, and I think they want us to hang on to each other and make 'em proud."

"All right, then. You can be my mama too."

He was steady sawing logs when Dobey laid him beside his baby brother Brick.

CHAPTER TWELVE

Dobey

"Mama, y'all should be fine here. Jimmy and I are just gonna get them to Hays. Once they're on that eastbound train, we'll be right back." Dobey gave the children a head rub, hugged Honey, and swung into the saddle.

Annette shielded her eyes against the rising sun with her one hand. "I ain't worried about us. We got Doc, Tad, Cherokee Jim, George Canada, and Big William to watch over us. It's you and Jimmy Melton I'm concerned about. Just the two of you, and that long trip back? And what about them two wagons?"

"They belong to the Count, Mama. He offered us a deal on 'em, but we've got two already. We'll just sell 'em there. Jimmy and I will try to hook up with soldiers heading back this way."

Melton pulled his horse up beside Dobey's

and caught the end of the conversation. He said, "Main thing is, Mama Balliett, you know we can't just let the Count and O'Reilly take Janey and Willi up there by themselves. And, 'sides that, me 'n Dobey needs to sniff around and see if anybody's seen Penn or Red."

They crossed the South Canadian and headed north, a half-hour after sunrise. It began to rain.

Melton

As they rode past Fort Hays heading into Hays City, Melton noticed that the fort looked empty. "Where you suppose all them Bluecoats is, Dobey?"

Dobey said, "I heard in Dodge City that the Seventh Cavalry had been split up and sent to Kentucky and the Carolinas."

"Occupation duty," snorted Melton.

Dobey smiled. "They call it, 'reconstruction', but you're more than likely right."

Melton said, "Anyways, ain't likely we'll run up on Penn, if the Seventh is gone. Leastways we oughtn't to bump into no Pinkertons either, seeing as how you buried us here first time we come up this way."

O'Reilly heard that last comment and said, "Beg pardon?"

Dobey grinned at him. "Yep. Y'all find out

the train schedule, and if we have time I'll take you up to Boot Hill to see our graves. Me and Boss are gonna stop in here at Bitter's Saloon and see if Hickok's back, and if Old John Bitter knows where Penn might be. Or Red."

"That, and have a drink," said Melton. "I guess dead men can do that."

"*Ach,*" said the Count, from the lead wagon. "Perhaps before you begin your celebration, you could point me to the *Bahnhof*? The train station, that is?"

"There ain't one," said Melton. "You might as well come on in Bitter's place with us. We'll ask him 'bout the train."

"Good plan," said O'Reilly. "We'll share a wee one, while we gather information."

"*Gnau,*" said the Count. "Exactly."

"Good," said Janey Green as she clambered down from the Count's wagon. "Mayhaps misters Melton and Walls can relax somewhat."

Count Baranov nodded toward the two men, as they stared holes in every man on the wet street. "*Nicht gnau,*" he said. "Not exactly."

"*Nein,*" said Willi. "*Neimals.* Never happen."

115

■ ■ ■ ■

1875

■ ■ ■ ■

CHAPTER THIRTEEN

Dobey

"I remember you. Masterson, right? You stopped by here after that Comanche attack on Adobe Walls last year. Some folks think I'm named for that place." Dobey stuck out his hand, and the slender dark-haired visitor took it.

"Yessir, Mister Walls. I remember that about you. I go by Bat."

"Call me Dobey. This here's my partner, Boss Melton."

The three men stood in the café inside the mud fort known as Balliett's Post. It was the largest structure in the growing community of Canadian Fort.

A large Negress approached from the kitchen. "Does y'all want some coffee, Mistuh Dobey? Food won't be ready for a couple hours yet, but I could cut some ham and bread fo' yo' guest."

Masterson shook his head, and said, "No

food, thanks. I ate on the way here."

Dobey said, "Coffee, then?"

When Masterson looked confused, Melton said, "Dobey's mama don't let us sell no liquor this side of the river. What we oughta do, Dobey, is take him over to Hogtown. We'll have a drink and catch up on the news. Doc'll want to hear it anyways." Melton gave Masterson a shrewd look. "Might be this youngster needs to have his tensions relieved, too."

Masterson grinned. "I stopped off there and took care of that problem before coming here. And I been thinking about Big William's cooking since my last visit. That's where I ate, but I sure don't mind going back."

Ten minutes later, the three men rode out through the gate, and Cherokee Jim closed it behind them. As they headed toward the crossing, a girl's voice stopped them. It came from the northwest tower.

"Daddy! Daddy! They's two wagons and a rider coming from the back thataway!" Dobey's nine year old daughter Millie pushed open a wooden shutter and pointed south.

The men rode to the corner under the tower and looked south. There were several click-snaps as three telescopes covered the newcomers.

"Don't know 'em," said Masterson. "The man's well-armed. Two belt pistols and a Yellowboy across his lap. Looks like pommel holsters too. A ranger, maybe?"

"Taught him well," Melton said. "That there is none other than Sheriff Buck Watson out of Jacksboro. Used to ride with us."

Dobey said, "Yep, and that's Junebug and some darky child in the first wagon. Don't know the darky woman driving the second one. Millie!" he yelled at the tower. "Get Black Dog to take over from you, and run tell your mama and grandma that Buck and Junebug has come home. We'll ride to meet 'em."

There was a porch with tables and benches attached to the café, and the cover, or "ramada" as Carmela called it, gave the crowd some relief from the June sun.

The cook yelled at her helper. "George. George Canada. Bring the folks some cool water and something to drink it from."

As the big black man moved silently through the press of chattering people passing out cups, Dobey started the introductions.

"Buck, Junebug, y'all know everybody

'cept our guest here. This is Bat Masterson. He was one of the buffalo hunters that drove off all those Comanches a year ago over at Adobe Walls. Bat, this is Sheriff Buck Watson and his woman, Junebug." He paused. "I don't think I've met your travelling friends."

Buck said, "That there is Mary Johnson and her daughter Cherry. Her husband Britt was kilt by Kioways four years back, and they been with us since. She's a good cook." He turned to Masterson. "I have heard some tales about yore fight. Maybe twenty-five of you held off a thousand Comanches, right?"

Masterson laughed. "I heard that too. All I saw was two or three hundred, but that sure seemed like a gracious plenty to me. Now, ain't you the lawman who killed seven or eight men with a pistol and a knife?"

"It was only five," said Buck. "I had two pistols and I kind of startled them. And I think Cap'n Dobey and Boss Melton was shooting too."

"He damn sure startled 'em," said Melton. "Yelled right in their faces and shot 'em to pieces. I'm gonna get a jug from my room, Dobey, if y'all want to meet me around back. Tell your mama not to look."

The men met in the shade of the blacksmith shop. Cherokee Jim and Dobey's brother Tad joined them, but declined the jug.

As soon as Buck took a swig, Melton said, "Well?"

Buck wiped the mouth of the jug with his kerchief, "Well, Boss, I'm looking for work. Gamblers said I was too hard on the rough crowd. Cowboys didn't want to quit shootin' up the place. What tore it was, I shot this soldier boy. He'd cut up one of our whores, and then he come at me. The Cap'n out at the fort said he's gonna put the whole town off limits, so the mayor fired me."

After a bit, Dobey said, "Seems like you could have stayed on there and made it just running your bar. Buckaroo Club, right?"

"Junebug sold it to Bow Legs Annie and Hannity. She just wanted me out of there." Buck reached for the jug again.

Nobody said anything for a minute. Finally, Buck said, "Seems there was talk about having me kilt. Junebug and Mary Johnson said we couldn't have that, not from no back-shooting gamblers, so here we is."

Tad reached for the jug, then passed it to Cherokee Jim. It was quiet for another minute, as the men sipped, and then the jug passed back to Melton. He took a big swallow.

"We could load up right now, ride down there and get your job back. Run off every damn one of them mealy-mouthed sonsabitches."

The jug made the round again.

Buck swallowed and wiped his mouth. "Junebug knowed you was gonna say that, Boss. She says she won't go back, no matter what."

After a bit, Masterson said, "Tell you what. I'm done scouting for the Army. There is a new town growing up around Hidetown, down to Sweetwater Creek. I'm heading there. I hear there's a hundred people there already. I bet they need some law."

Dobey said, "They call it Sweetwater. And I think they're starting up another fort there."

Masterson said, "That's what I hear too. Thought I might try gambling. Anyways, I know some of the Rath and Hanrahan people who's running it. They ran Adobe Walls. I'll tell 'em what I know about you, Buck."

Buck said, "Why'd you do that?"

"Hell, you're gonna open a bar and whorehouse, right? Maybe you'll hire me as your gambler. And I sure would like some company on the trip there."

Supper sobered the men up some, so afterwards Melton said to Dobey, "Your turn." When Dobey returned with a fresh jug, the men returned to the smithy.

Melton said, "Well, Buck, did you ask Junebug about this Sweetwater plan?"

Buck said, "I don't have to do that no more." He turned to Masterson. "So — I guess them buffalo guns is what drove off them Comanches?"

Masterson took a pull. "Those were real nice when they pulled away, but what won it for us was that most every one of us had conversion cartridge revolvers that we bought right here. When they got up close and tried to knock down the doors or shoot through our firing ports, we blistered 'em with those pistols. The two main buildings was sod, see, and we was close enough to sort of shoot 'em off each other. And we had a shotgun, and three repeaters. A Spencer and two Henrys."

"And, like you said, when they pulled away . . ."

Masterson thumped the table. "Then they were like buffalos, and we had at least twenty-five long guns. Sharps, Remingtons, Trapdoors, most of 'em fifty's or better. I think it was the third day, they'd pulled back a good ways and Billy Dixon took a .44-105 Sharps and knocked one of 'em off his horse."

Dobey said, "So, what's special about that?"

Masterson said, "Well, they were on a butte, see, most of a mile distant. Figgered they was safe. Billy still says it was a lucky shot that did it, but after that shot, they just left. It was like it broke their spirit."

"How many did you lose?"

Masterson thought for a moment. "We started with twenty-eight men, counting storekeepers and skinners. And Billy Olds' wife. The Shadler brothers were caught outside and killed along with their dog, right at first. Billy Tyler was my good friend and he got shot trying to save our horses. Fred Leonard pulled him inside, but he bled out. Lung shot." Masterson lost his voice for a few seconds.

When he could talk again, he said, "Only other one we lost was Billy Olds, the storekeeper, and it was after the fight. He went up a ladder to the roof to look around after they pulled away and took a Sharps Fifty up with him. Thought he seen the hostiles coming back. Cocked that carbine, then went to climb down with it, and caught the trigger on one of the rungs. Blew the top of his head off, and his wife reaching to help him down." Masterson stopped again to shake his head. "What he'd seen was another buffalo runner riding in. He told us he hadn't seen any Indians coming in. We was in the clear. Wasn't no reason for Billy to die."

Dobey said, "I don't know why they didn't hit us too."

Masterson said, "Hell, Mister Walls, I'm dead certain y'all was gonna be next. Only there wasn't no next."

CHAPTER FOURTEEN

Penn

The stage rumbled to a halt at Twenty-Mile Station, and five of the six passengers climbed out the left door to head inside for food, or around back to the privy. Penn stepped out the right side and kept an eye out for the station master. He spoke to the stage driver.

"Old Man Livengood still running this station?"

The driver replied, "Yep, him and his son, most times. 'Cept his son was back in Santy Fe, holed up with Mexican Sue. His most favorite whore."

Penn smiled and said, "Good for him." He thought, *Good for me.* "Guess I got time to visit the privy?"

"You do," said the driver, "Though you'll likely be last in line. Me and the guard got to change out that second right-hand mule.

Gone a little gimpy on us. Maybe half an hour?"

Penn said, "The station man don't help you?"

"Nah," said the driver. "His hands is full passing out bread and soup to you folks. Maybe selling a few shots of bust-head. You want to help?"

Penn laughed. "I would really like that, above all things. But I got a date with that little house out back."

Penn went uphill fast, past the little house and the three men still waiting to use it. A grizzled old miner said, "Where you heading, Ace?"

Penn pointed uphill. "All I needs is to piss. I'll go behind them rocks, in case some lady appears."

"A lady? Out here? You ain't from around here, is you, Ace?" The other men laughed.

Penn muttered, "Not for long, I'm not." He picked up a stick and jammed it up under the ledge where he'd stashed his slicker five years earlier. No rattler. He pulled out the slicker, shook two scorpions from it, and found the cash and the little pistol in the pockets as he'd left them.

He broke open the Smith and Wesson, cleared the empty shells and produced six new .32 rimfire cartridges from his shirt

129

pocket. Fresh loaded, it went in his coat pocket and Penn walked back downhill. He waited by the back of the station house until the other passengers were loading the stage, then ducked inside.

Livengood was collecting soup bowls and tin cups and dropping them into a large wash basin. He looked up but didn't recognize the heavily bearded Penn, who was also much more lean than he'd been on his last visit, when Livengood wounded and captured him. Five damn years ago.

"Them others done finished the soup," Livengood said, over his shoulder. "They's some bread on the table, and a shot of that liquor is two bits."

Penn said, "That's fine. You need any help?"

Livengood said, "Not really. Say, I know that voice. I don't never forget one. You been here before. Do I know you?" He put the basin on the floor under the pump head and started to turn to look at his visitor. Too late.

Penn stepped behind him and pulled Livengood's own knife from its sheath. He grabbed a handful of the station master's hair, yanked his head back and cut his throat.

Penn rode him down and knelt on his

130

back, pushing away from the blood spray as the man kicked, gurgled and died.

He found a stash of about forty dollars in Livengood's pocket, grabbed a half loaf of bread and the whiskey bottle and ran to the stage.

"That blood on yore laig?" yelled the driver, as Penn scrambled in.

"Yessir," shouted Penn from inside. "That old fool cut hisself with his own knife. Swore he didn't need no help, though. I asked him. He did give us some bread and liquor. We'll pass you up some in a minute."

The driver snapped the reins and they pulled away. He looked sideways at his shotgun rider and said, "Look back and see is old Livengood running after us. You know that boy stole that stuff. Old Livengood ain't never give nothing to nobody. 'Cept maybe the pox."

CHAPTER FIFTEEN

Dobey

After his noon bowl of chili, Dobey headed for the northwest tower to check on the children on watch there. He barely left the kitchen when his eleven year old son Tommy Christmas rushed halfway down the ladder, then jumped clear and ran full steam at him, shouting, "Papa Dobey! Papa Dobey!"

"Easy, Son. What's got you in an uproar?" Dobey took a calming stance, but was concerned because Tommy was usually unflappable himself.

"Wagons, Papa Dobey, a bunch of wagons. Coming from down that way."

"A bunch of them? What kind of report is that?"

"Yessir. I mean three of 'em. Two big ones, one buckboard. And Millie spotted 'em first. And two riders. And I've seen some of 'em before, but I don't remember no names."

Melton stepped out of the kitchen, wiping his mouth with his kerchief. "What's the commotion?"

Dobey said, "Young'uns has spotted three wagons and two riders coming from the south. Says some of 'em is familiar looking, but he can't call any names."

Melton said, "I'll go glass 'em. You gonna tell Big William to keep the cook fire going?"

Dobey said, "I'll do that." He rubbed Tommy's head and said, "Good report. Go back up with Uncle Boss and tell your sister I said she done good."

Minutes later, Dobey climbed the tower to have a look-see himself. Melton passed him the telescope and said, "You ain't gonna believe this. I reckon they do look some familiar. Look who's driving that buckboard."

Dobey squinted a moment, then said, "Is that Junebug?"

Melton nodded. "Sure is. And I'll kiss your butt on Sunday morning if that ain't her mankiller lawman husband on that strawberry roan off to the left."

Dobey swung the scope and said, "Buck Watson. It surely is."

Melton jabbed a finger at the approaching convoy. "And that ain't all. Study that feller on the first big wagon. Try and see him without that little mustache."

Dobey's head popped up. "Willi? The Count's boy Willi?"

"Damn sure is," said Melton. "Don't know who that is riding alongside him. It ain't the Count. Looks like some young Mexican cavalry officer, with his green coat and gold buttons and all."

He was not a Mexican, though he was a former cavalry officer. He was a huge, hard man, and very Prussian, and named Konrad Lang. A major, according to Willi, who introduced him as his special friend. The third wagon was managed by two more Prussians, former noncoms who spoke little English.

"What're you doing here, then, Junebug? Did Buck run out of hard cases to kill?" Melton grinned and nudged Dobey as he spoke.

Junebug said, "When Willi come through Sweetwater, Buck spotted him, and Willi said he'd pay us to lead him and his soldier boys up here. We'd been thinking on it anyways, and here we is. Thought we'd visit a while, then go back to Sweetwater."

Dobey swung to face Willi. "Speaking of you, Willi, are you here to visit or to stay? Looks like you got enough baggage to make a stay of it. And how's His Majesty The Count doing?"

Willi said, "I am sorry to tell you, my father the Count Baranov, is dead." Everyone groaned. Willi continued, "He was good so as to acknowledge me. And to leave to me and to Janey a great much of money. She has gone back to her old home to buy it back, and I have come here to buy some land and some cows."

"Cattle," said Konrad Lang. "I am thinking you are calling them cattle, and with the long horns. Not 'cows,' I think."

"*Ja, gnau,*" Willi said. "I mean, yes. Exactly. And we will call our place *Osterreich* Ranch."

Melton snorted. "Ostrich Ranch? You naming it for some dumb-assed African bird?"

"*Nicht gnau,*" said Willi. "*Osterreich.* Austria. Mine homeland. It is to respect my country."

Melton smiled. "Good luck with that."

Melton

Ostrich Ranch blossomed quickly. "That happens," Melton explained to Manuela, "when you got a man with more money than brains. And it don't hurt when you got so many folks hereabouts that needs work.

135

And knows how to build these things. And knows where to find loose cattle."

Manuela made a funny face. "*Jaime,* my husband, I think you don' like Willi so much because he don' like girls, *si?*"

Dobey and Honey both laughed at this and pointed fingers at Jimmy Melton. The two couples were having coffee on the eating porch of the café on a cool morning.

Melton sat up straight, shook his head and jabbed a finger back at the others.

"Naw," he said, "that ain't so. Ain't no such thing. I was in the army since I's a boy, and the army is full of men like that. They knowed not to bother me and I didn't bother them. It sure don't mean they can't fight. Hell, some of the best officers and sergeants I've knowed didn't never care for women."

"He's right," said Dobey, as Manuela gave both men a doubting look. "I expect all armies has been that way, always. Sort of a haven. Not for the ones that choose to dress and act like women, of course."

Melton said, "I've give it some thought. I don't think they can help it. Seems to me it's how they's born. Leastways, the ones I've knowed."

Honey said, "Shelly says the Indians don't think anything of it. Says a few boys will be

136

more like girls and the tribes let 'em go their own way. Every young man don't have to be a warrior. And sometimes they's girls who don't like men, and some of them do ride and fight like men."

Melton said, "Go figure. Now don't get me wrong. I see some man trying to mess with some child, I'm gonna hurt him before I run him off. Or kill him."

"True," said Dobey, "But it wouldn't matter if the child was a girl or a boy. Same either way. That's a whole different story. That'd be one sick son of a gun, and one I'd just as soon put down."

The others nodded. Melton said, "I'll tell you something else. I don't think Willi is scared of much. I mean, he didn't have to come back out here. He has got more money than God, and this ain't no easy country. And if somebody wants to make light of his friend Major Lang, I 'spect they best be ready for a real scrap."

Manuela gave him an impish smile. "So, *Jaime,* you *do* like Willi. What kind of *gringo* have I married?"

Melton grinned and held up both hands. "It ain't hard to find out."

■ ■ ■ ■

1876

■ ■ ■ ■

CHAPTER SIXTEEN

Junebug

"Well, if it ain't Sergeant Oregano Jones. How you doing, White Buffalo?" Buck pushed away from the table and extended his hand as he stood.

Junebug remained seated but said, "Hey, Whitey. You bring Mary Johnson home?"

Sergeant Jones pulled off a glove to shake Buck's hand and nodded to Junebug.

"Yassum, Miz Junebug. She around back to her cabin. Say she tired."

Junebug caught a trace of a smile on the bronze face of the large negro soldier. "Well, what can we do you for? Drink? Some coffee on a cold January night?" Junebug genuinely liked the big man. Probably would have even if Mary Johnson wasn't sweet on him, but any friend of Mary's was going to be just fine with Junebug.

The sergeant said, "Drink sound good. Don't wanna cause y'all no trouble though, selling whiskey to a old darky. 'Specially on a night you s'posed to be closed."

Sweetwater's population was such that several of the saloon owners had decided to close one or two bars most nights and rotate the closings. The owners and girls got a break if they wanted it, and the drinkers and gamblers were concentrated in the open establishments. Gamblers, whores, and owners could go to someone else's bar if they didn't want a break, and the policy forced customers to occasionally try places other than their favorite watering hole. The Ring Town Saloon, built close to the fort for the buffalo soldiers, did not take part in the rotating closings.

"Who said anything about selling you a drink?" Buck poured two shots and pushed one toward Sergeant Jones. "Set yourself down, Whitey. You seem a little worked up."

Jones pulled off his battered gray hat and ran a hand through his fuzzy white hair. "Thankee," he said, and knocked back the drink. "Thing is, Buck, you kinda the only law around here. You know that little white sergeant, name of King?"

"I do," Buck said. "Used to work for Colonel MacKenzie, but now on detached duty, or some such. Seems like a good man."

"He is, when he sober. He ain't sober

tonight. I seen him on the street. He carrying his pistol, say he gonna kill some gambler that took his money and his woman."

Junebug said, "Did he say who?"

Jones shrugged. "Masters, maybe? Something like that."

Buck jumped up. "Lord, Junebug, that's got to be Masterson. I'll go see can I head him off. Can you come with me, Whitey?"

Jones stood. "Nossir. Don't know how long it would take, and I got a long patrol going out before daybreak. Ain't got much time to get the boys ready as it is. And I don't need to get between no white people fighting. Hell, they'd all start shooting at me."

A minute later, Junebug was alone. She locked up. Ten minutes later, someone tapped on the door, and she opened it to find Bat Masterson and the whore Mollie Brennan shivering on the porch. She hustled them in, looked up and down the street, and locked up again.

Bat grinned. "Glad you was awake. I took all Melvin King's money this evening, and then he saw me talking with Mollie and really got crossways. Good thing he wasn't carrying, or I mighta had to shoot him. Anyway, he was mouthing off about getting a gun, so I thought we'd barge in here and stay out of trouble 'til he sleeps it off."

Junebug said, "Well, he went and got his pistol and he's looking for you two. Buck went to try to head him off and warn you."

Mollie said, "Thanks for putting us up 'til this passes, Junebug. I hope he don't shoot Buck. You'd never forgive us."

"Ain't likely he'll get the drop on Buck. Lemme get you something to drink. Coffee or the hard stuff?"

Bat said, "Coffee," and Mollie nodded for some too.

Junebug took the pot off the stove and went behind the bar to get three mugs. There was another clatter at the door.

Bat said, "That'll be Buck. I got it."

As he opened the door, there was the blast of a pistol shot and Bat was knocked backward five feet and down on his back.

Sergeant Melvin King, five and a half feet of drunken scrawny meanness, stepped in through the gunsmoke, waving his long-barreled Colt .45. He cocked it again as Bat drew his little .38, and Mollie moved between them.

The men fired together. Bat, shooting from the floor, put his bullet in King's chest. King's big slug killed Mollie. King dropped his pistol and collapsed, and Junebug ran to Mollie.

"Lord, Bat, she's dead. Where are you hit?"

"Don't rightly know," he said. "Stomach maybe. My hip for sure. I hope I killed that mean little bugger. I sure don't want to play him no more cards."

Junebug picked up the big Army Colt and leaned over King. "He's still breathing, but not for long."

"Don't shoot him, Junebug. Let him die slow. I really liked that girl."

"Well, Bat, she took a bullet for you."

"You think so, Junebug? I mean, I think she liked me too, but you think she did that for me?"

"I'm sure of it, Bat. No question." *I just don't think she meant to. She was heading for the door.*

Sergeant King finally died the next afternoon.

When Buck told her of King's death, Junebug said, "Good. Mollie was a good whore and a good friend. She didn't deserve this."

Buck nodded. "Yep. Whore's life is a hard one."

"And just what the hell would you know about that, Buck Watson?"

"Durn, Junebug, did you just cuss?"

145

■ ■ ■ ■

Dobey

Four months after the Masterson-King fight, a bullwhacker from Dodge brought a message for Dobey from Hickok.

"Penn is back with the Seventh Cavalry," it said. "They're up around Fort Lincoln. I'm heading up that way to Deadwood. Word is, it is wide open for a sporting man. I hear any more on Penn I'll send word. Your servant, Wild Bill."

Dobey and Melton started packing that afternoon. Bear insisted on going with them.

"She was your wife, Boss, but long before that she was my mother. Me, I'm going. With or without you."

Shelly insisted on going with Bear. They left the next day.

CHAPTER SEVENTEEN

Monasetah

Most of the women in the huge encampment hated the job of scraping fat from the inside of animal hides. Monahsetah found it boring, of course, but she found that once she got into the rhythm, she could let her mind go elsewhere. Right now her mind was north of the river.

As she scraped and sweated in the June sun, Monahsetah felt joy that Weasel was over there, taking time to play father to her boy, who was sometimes badly treated by other Cheyenne children.

She and the other captive women had been hard used by Creeping Panther and his men, seven winters ago, but they hadn't been killed. They certainly hadn't been treated as rough as some Cheyenne prisoners were. Others in her tribe seemed to resent that Creeping Panther had selected her and kept her for himself for months even though she'd been seven months pregnant with Black Butterfly. Of course later they resented Creeping Panther's son, Yellow Bird. And she knew in her heart who Yellow Bird's father was, even though she had often been forced to submit to Creeping Panther's brother Tom. That was just another one of many strange White customs.

Even her childhood friend Striker had said, "You should have killed yourself, instead of sleeping with those yellow-haired devils." Striker had always been sweet on Monahsetah, but she had turned him down along with all the other warriors who had tried to take her as a wife. She knew, deep in her soul, that Creeping Panther would come back to her, for her, someday.

She rocked back on her heels, and set the scraping tool on a nearby flat rock. She wiped her forehead and smiled at Black Butterfly as she played with the smaller children they were caring for. Killing herself would also have taken the unborn life of this beautiful, loving daughter.

What did Striker know, anyhow? Hadn't she used her influence with Creeping Panther to get all the captive women and children, over fifty of them, released?

She had told Striker, and others too, to go suck eggs. She smiled to herself and reached for the scraping tool. To her amazement, it began to dance on the flat rock, then fell off before she could grab it.

Monahsetah felt the pounding before the other nearby women did because she was kneeling beside the deer hide, while the others stood and chattered. She knew immediately what the vibrations were. This was the year that the Whites called 1876 and the buffalo herds, what was left of them, were nowhere near the Valley of the Greasy Grass. It could only be horses running.

"I believe the horses have been scared," she said to the other women. She stood, shielded her eyes against the summer sun, and stared at the ridge to the southwest where the herd grazed. Thousands of horses were there, looking like worms crawling all over the ridge; restive, maybe, but raising no dust. Not running. Then she heard the trumpet. She began to run.

The first gunshots and screams were drowned out by her yelling. She stuffed her knife, scraping tool, and awl into her parfleche and yelled at her daughter, "Black Butterfly! Gather the children. Help me. We must rush across the river. Hurry, daughter. The Long Knives are coming. They are coming again!"

■ ■ ■ ■

Black Butterfly

Black Butterfly froze, staring at her mother. For as long as she could hear and understand in her eight summers, her mother had told her of the Dawn of the Long Knives, when Creeping Panther and his Bluecoats had overrun Black Kettle's village along the Lodge Pole River far to the south. Black Butterfly herself had been there, but still in Monahsetah's womb. Her mother's father had died in that fight along with about twelve other warriors and maybe twelve women and six children.

The screams, shouting and crackle of gunfire from up the valley touched her deep in her subconscious and gave her goose bumps in the scorching summer heat. Had she heard those sounds and registered them, sensed her mother's fear, two months before she came into the world?

A bee zinged by her head. There was a thud and a grunt, and Black Butterfly turned toward Old Woman Walks Fast, an old Arapahoe woman who helped Black Butterfly with the children. Old Woman Walks Fast clutched her chest and stumbled backwards, falling into the entrance of a tipi.

Monahsetah was gathering the smaller children and shoving them toward the river and still shouting at Black Butterfly. The words would not come through Black Butterfly's ears.

"Mother, there are bees everywhere. One has stung Old Woman Walks Fast. We must help her."

Monahsetah grabbed her daughter's shoulders and shook her. "Those are bullets. Listen to me. We have talked of this. We must take the children we are caring for and go to the river. Now. RUN."

The camp exploded. There were three fording sites in the valley of the Little Bighorn. Hundreds of warriors grabbed weapons and ran to face the Long Knives charging down the valley from the south ford. Hundreds more mounted and followed Crazy Horse to get between the Whites and the pony herd.

Many more rode and ran to the central crossing, near the north end of the village. Black Butterfly, her mother, and the children ran with this group.

Striker

The Long Knives coming from the south crossing had opened their charge at least two rifle shots distant from the village, giving Striker and other warriors just enough time to react.

Striker ran through the Lakota lodge circles to join many other Cheyenne and Lakota warriors to place themselves in a dry creek bed between the camp and the enemy. They began firing as the Bluecoats came within a quarter mile. Some of the warriors had Yellow-boys, the model '66 Winchesters; more had old Spencers, Henrys and Sharps. A few had Enfields, and about half had only bows and arrows. Striker and several others had the newer, more powerful '73 Winchesters. The rapid fire of this force stopped the cavalry charge cold, except for two troopers whose horses bolted directly into the camp; they were pulled down and hacked to death, one of them not ten strides from Striker.

The other soldiers dismounted and began a brisk counter fire with their carbines. Their single shot .45-70 Trapdoors were no match for the Indians' repeaters for speed, but had greater power and range. Many of their shots sailed over Striker's head and deep into the camp behind him. He knew those bullets were taking a toll on the old people, women, and children still milling about and yelling back there, and it made his heart hard.

Another cry arose from behind him and soon spread to the firing line. "Crazy Horse is coming! Crazy Horse is coming!" Lakota women were trilling all through the camp, and the warriors also began to roar as the slender Oglala fighter, a lightning flash painted across his face, rode out to the right to a slight hill in front of the pony herd. Following him were hundreds of mounted warriors — all the Lakota tribes, of course, the Oglala, Brule, Minneconjou, Huncpapa, Blackfeet, Two Kettle, and Sans Arc, but also Southern and Northern Cheyenne.

Out-gunned and badly out-numbered, the Bluecoats moved into some trees along the river and briefly attempted a stand there.

Striker moved with other fighters who worked their way into the trees to the left of the Bluecoats. Forty paces away, Striker saw one of the hated Indian scouts on horseback, talking to a mounted officer. Striker sent a flat-nosed .44-40 toward the back of the Indian's head.

"I hope he was an Osage," he thought, as he knelt and began pushing more cartridges into the carbine's loading gate. As the smoke from his shot cleared, he saw the scout down, his horse fleeing and the blood-spattered officer scrambling to dismount, then remount and ride away. Most of the soldiers followed him. Some were left behind.

Some of these had lost their mounts in the melee; some stumbled or were just slow. Some of these were quickly cut down and left to die slowly. Horribly. Striker scalped the scout he'd killed, noting that he was an old Arikara. *Can't find any Osage to kill up here,* he thought, as he scrambled to capture a cavalry horse and then joined the chase as the Bluecoats began a frantic run, out of the woods and back upriver.

When the Oglala Crazy Horse saw the Bluecoats start to flee, he led the larger force of warriors guarding the ponies to attack the soldiers from across the plain. They charged into the Bluecoats' flank and pushed them over to the river, far short of the ford. The soldiers followed their leader and jumped their horses into the deep river, more than a tall man's height below, their bellies smacking like gunshots as they hit the water. They then fought to get through the one exit, a narrow cut in the far bank.

Striker reined in on the river bank and yelled at the Bluecoats as he fired into their floundering ranks. "Not so easy this time, hunh? You are like buffalos. Why didn't you ride back to the ford? You are crazy!" He shot an officer off his horse, and when the wounded man grabbed another soldier's stirrup to be pulled from the fast water, Striker shot him loose.

Crazy Horse was everywhere, counting coups and screaming the Lakota war cry, "Hoka Hey!" Striker thought, *He really is crazy.*

Dog Soldiers rode up and shouted that more Bluecoats were circling the main camp. Most of the warriors, Cheyenne and Lakota alike, followed Crazy Horse and melted away to protect the village. Thinking of his mother and Monahsetah, Striker rode back with them.

As he crossed the plain, he came upon a cluster of women and boys around a wounded black man sitting by his dead horse. The Huncpapa chief Sitting Bull was there too, and he said, "It's old Teat. He's an Indian talker for the Bluecoats, but he has a Huncpapa wife. Leave him alone." Sitting Bull gave the man some water and rode off.

Striker knew the talker by his White name of Dorman. Dorman said, "I'm dying. Don't torture me."

A Huncpapa woman said, "Well, Teat, you shouldn't have come with these Whites to attack us, and kill my little brother. He was only ten summers." She fired her pistol into his head and the other women fell on him with their knives and hatchets.

The Bluecoats had lost several men in their flight to the river. Striker had never cared for the women's butchery tradition. It made his balls tingle. As he hurried back to camp he saw more of it. A lot of it. He prayed aloud, "Ma'heo'o, don't let me be taken alive. At least not by women like these."

CHAPTER EIGHTEEN

John Boye

Several miles south, Captain Benteen stopped his command. "Let the men dismount and stretch," he grunted as he swung out of the saddle. "He's sent me on a wild goose chase, the bugger. We'll turn here and angle back to catch him. He wants to do it all by himself."

Sergeant Boye knew who Benteen referred to, and why. The enmity between Benteen and Lieutenant Colonel Custer was long-standing and common knowledge.

Their old Crow scout sighed. Boye winked at him and said, "Here we go again."

"How come you hate him so, Colonel Benteen?" asked another scout, who was on his first campaign with the Seventh Cavalry. Like most soldiers, he called Benteen by his brevet rank.

"I've despised him since he left Joel Elliot and those boys to be slaughtered on the

Washita." Benteen's face darkened as his voice rose. "Didn't ride to their aid, then didn't even go get their bodies. Left 'em for the Cheyenne women to cut 'em up. The bastard. I was there when we went back for 'em, two weeks later. It was awful to behold."

"Aye, it was, too," said Boye, his Color Sergeant. "Cut to shreds, they was, frozen stiff, heads an' hands cut off, along of their private parts. Shot full of arrows too, and left face down."

A new lieutenant hesitated, then chimed in. "But sir, the General is no coward. Surely you do not mean he acted timidly."

Benteen glared at him. "I've never said the man was a coward. Never. He has balls as big as cannon shells, as you'll see if we get into a fight. But he's a God-damned glory hound, always was. That's why he didn't ride to help Elliott's command or recover their bodies. He'd had a happy little fight, only lost a few men, took prisoners and killed six or seven hundred ponies, and he didn't want to spoil it. If we'd ventured another two miles downriver to where Elliott and Sergeant Major Kennedy were, we'd have been in a real fight."

Color Sergeant Boye spat. "Too right, sir.

158

Prob'ly a half dozen other villages down there."

Benteen remounted. "And that's why he's sent us out here, too. Wants to find and take another village without me. I've never let him nor anyone else forget Elliott and the Washita.

"Color Sergeant Boye, mount 'em up and let us go at a trot."

They soon cut Custer's trail, and stopped at a boggy water hole to water the horses and refill canteens. As the men and horses milled around the swampy area, the D Company commander, Captain Weir, rode up and accused Benteen of lollygagging, then took his company on up Custer's well-beaten path to the north.

John Boye said, "Don't let him get to you, Colonel Benteen. You know he's one of the Boy General's fair-haired officers. He's just mad 'cause you pushed Custer to send his company with us. And he wants to be with the General when he finds that village and sweeps through it like a hot knife through butter. Hell, sir, so do you."

Benteen swung into the saddle. "I only asked for him because Custer has favored him with the best-manned company in the regiment. I didn't appreciate being sent out with three understrength companies to

159

search endless little valleys for a 'huge hostile village.' Let's ride. I want to catch and pass the snotty bastard."

Benteen and Boye soon retook the lead from D Company, and were themselves overtaken by a lone rider. "Here comes the General's brother Boston, Colonel. The boy's a civilian forager 'cause his consumption keeps him from being a soldier. I talked with him some back at Fort Lincoln." Boye waved to the man who slowed to a trot as he passed them. Custer's brother shouted a greeting.

"Afternoon, Colonel, John Boye. Going to join my brothers. I can't stand the dust and foot dragging back there with the ammunition train. They are maybe a mile or two behind you, but the mules were allowed to blunder into that bog, and now they're thoroughly mired. I'll see you at the village." He doffed his hat and kicked his horse back into a canter.

Benteen grunted. "Well, now the General will have his whole family with him. Both brothers, Tom and this one, and Lieutenant Calhoun's his brother-in-law. And never forget his nephew, young Autie Reed. He'll need them, if he's right about us going against fifteen hundred hostiles. This won't be like the Washita, with us taking on a hundred warriors with seven hundred men. And he's split us again."

John Boye nodded. "That worked back then, against a small camp. Don't you think this time he'll just try to find and hold them? Wait for the other two wings?"

Benteen snorted. "Him? Wait? Do you make sport? Now, what's this?"

Another lone rider approached, but from their front. Sergeant Daniel Kanipe trotted up, waving his hat.

"We've struck a big village downstream, Colonel Benteen. A few more miles and you hit the river. The village is a few miles after that, but on the other side. The General wants you to come on fast. And I'm to find the ammunition train and hurry them along too."

John Boye said, "They're a mile or so back, Danny, my lad."

Kanipe rode off, shouting, "We've got 'em now, boys. They're licking the stuffing out of 'em."

As the troops cheered, Benteen said, "We'll maintain a fast walk. We've a ways to go, and sounds like the fun's already over." Another mile passed and another rider appeared from their front, this one galloping in from the hills to their right, his horse all lathered. And bleeding.

Boye said, "My God, sir, it's John Martin, the trumpeter that Custer took this morning. He's jumping out'n his skin. We ain't ever gonna understand a word he says. You know he's an Eye-talian, fresh off the boat, and his real name is Joe Vanny Martini, or sump'n like that."

The trumpeter saluted Benteen and passed him a note, then laughed nervously and said, "Itsa froma de General, see?"

Benteen read it and handed it to Sergeant Boye. It said, "Benteen. Come on. Big village. Be quick. Bring pack. W.W. Cooke. PS bring pacs." Captain Weir joined them, and John Boye passed him the note.

Weir said, "By God, Adjutant Cooke is excited, I'd say. Misspelling and repeating himself. Not like him. Well, Benteen, we must push on."

Benteen took back the note, looked at it again, and tucked it in a saddle bag. "I don't know if he wants me to hurry or go back and bring the ammunition packs. Where is Custer, Martin?"

"Abouta t'ree mile froma here." He went on in his thick accent to say that the General had probably already charged through the village by now, and that Major Reno was charging the camp too, and killing men, women, and children right and left.

Benteen sent word to the pack train to hurry, and led out at a trot. He soon was faced with a second dilemma. A large body of horsemen had gone straight ahead, down toward the valley, while a larger body had veered to the right, off over the rolling hills. After some discussion, Weir took his company straight and the other three companies went right. Benteen and John Boye rode between the two groups. At the sound of heavy gunfire from the bluffs to the right, Weir's company rejoined, and the battalion formed a line and broke into a gallop. They soon closed on Major Reno's battalion digging in on a bluff above the river.

Major Reno, a red scarf around his head, rode up to Benteen and shouted, "For God's sake, Benteen, halt your command and help me. I've lost half my men. We are whipped."

As the officers talked, Sergeant Boye found Sergeant Daniel. "What the hell happened, James? And who is down there across the river?" He handed Daniel his canteen, and noticed the man's bloody arm.

"And that was us, Johnny. Thankee." He drank, then wiped the canteen rim before handing it back. "The major ordered a charge a couple of miles from the camp and the damn horses was blown out and gasping before we got there. We never made it."

"Didn't you, now?"

"Never we did. Hundreds of the red bastards riz up and shot the bloody hell out of us. We skirmished, then pulled into some woods along the river, tried to make a stand, and we was doing all right there." Daniel took a breath. "Then the major jumped on his horse and without so much as a never-you-mind, he takes off back this way."

"This way, you say. Not to the ford?"

Daniel spat. "Damn." He coughed. "Lungs is full of dust. No, Johnny. Maybe we was heading there but hundreds more of 'em charged us from across the valley and pushed us to the river, right down there, the bottom of this hill. We crossed back over under heavy fire. Water was deep and fast, and the banks was steep. Lost a bunch of men and officers there, too. We been holding 'em off here ever since. They pulled away some as you come up."

"And our illustrious leader, James, where the hell is he? He didn't support you?"

"Lieutenant Hodgson said the General was going to follow us into the village, but he didn't. Poor bugger, I seen Hodgson shot off his horse in the river, then shot loose from a man trying to pull him out. Some of the boys think they seen Custer up here, on

164

this here hill or that next one, as we was making our charge. Some Crow scouts with him, and waving his hat and pointing downstream, like he was gonna go around and hit 'em from the other side."

"Too right, James, he never crossed. We followed his trail from the ford to near here, then we heard you fighting and swerved over to come to you. No, the Boy General is up ahead somewheres, on this side. He sent two riders, one with a note to Colonel Benteen, telling him to come on with the ammunition packs. Big village, lots of Indians, he said. Colonel Benteen says he can't do both. Hurry, you know, and bring the pack train too."

"He don't know the half of it. Johnny, you ain't never seen so many tents and horses and Indians and goddamn Winchesters. Y'all ain't going after him, are you, Johnny? Y'all need to stay here, dig in with us. Maybe, with y'all and the ammunition packs, we can hold 'em off."

Sergeant Boye shrugged. "I ain't in charge, am I now? So, James. Still happy you left H Company for that extry stripe in M Company?"

"Didn't want to, but I didn't wanna stay a corporal forever. I'll tell you this, John Boye. Major Reno ain't no Colonel Benteen, for certain sure. I'm glad Benteen is here. I think Reno's drunk. And I wish I was too. Might not be so fornicating scared."

Sergeant Boye looked over at the officers' conference. "Don't you think Reno and Benteen will take us to Custer?"

"I hopes not, Johnny. These damn carbines is overheating, and the copper empties is getting stuck in the chambers. You needs a knife to pry 'em out, then you loads, shoots, and do it again. They's too many Indians. They had us three or four to one, and there was more riding away. They wasn't running, Johnny. They was heading to meet Custer, I guess."

Boye dismounted and pulled Daniel close. "No more of your God-damned exaggerations here, Sergeant Daniel, my boy. Those cartridges is fine, long as they's clean. You can talk that shite in the canteen, and it's all fine as you please, but not now, not here. Most of these boys look half-panicky, as it is."

Daniel took Boye's hand and pushed it away. "I ain't built it up none, Color Sergeant, and I ain't drunk. Y'all go on and help the General, if you please. But if you goes, leave me your tobaccy."

"Why would I do that, James?"

" 'Cause you ain't gonna need it."

CHAPTER NINETEEN

Monahsetah

"Take the older children across, then come back and help me with these younger ones." Monahsetah had to yell over the cries of the children and the shouting in the Cheyenne camp behind her.

Black Butterfly nodded, still in shock, and started to splash across the shallow central ford. The water caused her pale yellow dress to turn darker, a sharp contrast with her raven-black hair.

Before Monahsetah could yell for help with the smaller ones, a dozen of their mothers and aunts ran up. They threw down the turnips they'd been digging and started the herd of children across.

As Monahsetah slogged across carrying two babies, she looked up to see Weasel and her son Yellow Bird running down the hill toward them. Two coulees, or dry ravines, met on the far side of the crossing. Deep

Coulee flowed down from the left, and Medicine Tail from the right. Weasel and Yellow Bird were two hundred yards up the right side.

"Which way now, Mother?"

"Your brother is coming to help us, Black Butterfly. Take them up to the right. Do you see him?"

Her daughter nodded, grabbed two six-year olds by the wrist and began running. The brassy sound of a trumpet brought them to a staggering halt. This horn was somewhere in front of them.

Weasel faced about, knelt, and began firing his Spencer back up the coulee. The ground began to tremble again.

Their colored banner flapping, pistols waving, a troop of Long Knives on gray horses thundered into view. Weasel shot one soldier off his horse and killed the horse of a sergeant before he was ridden down.

As Monahsetah and the other women screamed at the children to go back into the village, Yellow Bird pitched face down, less than a hundred yards away. He struggled back to his hands and knees. He looked downhill at his mother and threw up.

Monahsetah handed the two babies to her daughter who was running back across the river. "Hurry," she screamed, then turned and sloshed toward her son. She fell, got up, and was knocked down by one of the huge gray horses. The sergeant riding it fired his revolver at her as she got up, missing but stinging her face with the powder. He then swatted her with the pistol.

She staggered, then grabbed the horse's tail and jammed her knife up under it. The horse screamed and bolted into the village. Monahsetah stumbled backwards several steps and fell again.

Sitting up, she watched two other soldiers ride to the edge of the river, fire into the village, then wheel away. Most of the soldiers had pulled up short of the river crossing. Monahsetah rolled over onto her knees, trying to clear the sparks and flashes from her brain and saw a Cheyenne warrior running directly at her from the village.

Striker snatched her to her feet, shoved her toward the camp and shouted, "Run," then snapped off two shots at the Bluecoats as they pulled back.

Monahsetah pushed by him, and when he tried to stop her, she slashed his arm. "Ai-iee," he shouted. "Are you crazy?"

Striker chased her. She struggled from the river, then began running and screaming her son's name. Yellow Bird was crawling down the right side of Medicine Tail Coulee toward them, over fifty steps away. Before Striker could react, a corporal carrying a colored banner rode over and fired his pistol at Yellow Bird's head. Monahsetah screamed and fell to her knees.

As the flag bearer spun his horse and cocked his pistol again, Striker shot him. The corporal dropped his pistol, arched his back and galloped off toward Deep Coulee. The other soldiers followed him. Cheyenne and Lakota warriors poured across the ford and pursued the soldiers, running and riding along both sides of the coulee and firing down into it.

Striker pulled Monahsetah to her feet and they ran up close to where Yellow Bird lay, but she dropped to her knees and crawled the last five steps, moaning incomprehensible mother-prayers. She cradled him, and her moans turned to wails.

Striker shifted his feet nervously. "I think he died trying to get to his mother and sister to protect them," he ventured.

"No," she spat at him. "He died, running to his mother, a scared boy. This was only his seventh summer, Striker." She wiped dark blood from her son's chin. "And do you know who killed him? Did you see the marks on that horse's flank?" She was shouting now.

"Yes," said Striker, cautiously. "The man with the flag killed him."

"The horse's mark. The white man's letters. The number seven, Striker. This was the Gray Horse Troop of the Seventh Cavalry. Creeping Panther's horsemen. Yellow Bird was killed by one of his own father's soldiers," she screamed, spittle running with her tears.

Striker nodded slowly, and looked up hill. Out of carbine range, on a ridge between Deep Coulee and Medicine Tail, a line of Bluecoat riders was moving north.

"His father wasn't at this little fight. You would have seen him," Striker said. "And the leader of the fight at the other end of the camp was a short fat man with dark hair. I was there. Creeping Panther must be up there, going to meet these men we just chased off. I will get my horse, and go up there and find him and shoot many holes in him."

He turned to re-cross the river, but she stopped him. "Don't forget Weasel," she said. "He's just up there a little ways. I think they wiped him out, but you'd better look."

Striker

Striker picked up the flag bearer's revolver and ran another forty steps up the side of

171

the coulee. Weasel was there, sprawled behind a bush, surrounded by empty cartridges. He'd been shot through his side and thigh, and his face was covered in blood.

As Striker bent to pick up Weasel's Spencer, the old man grabbed his wrist and sat up. "A gray horse attacked me. Kicked me in the head. I cannot see very well just now. Help me up," he groaned.

Striker handed the Spencer back to Weasel, and said, "Use this to lean on. I'll help you to the river. You can wash your eyes there."

"Striker, is that you? What are you doing here? Is Yellow Bird all right? Monahsetah will slap my ears if I don't get him back safe."

Striker stopped and took a deep breath. "Listen to me, Weasel. Yellow Bird is dead. The Long Knives killed him, and they belong to Creeping Panther. He's up there on that ridgeline somewhere. I'm going to get my horse and try to find him and kill him."

Weasel dropped his carbine and gripped Striker's arm, shuddering. "I'm out of bullets, I can't see, I can't run. I don't want to live. No. You must help me clean my eyes, find me a gun or more Spencer bullets, and let me ride with you. To avenge the boy."

"Come on. You can have this new Colt I just picked up. Still got four rounds in it."

As they shuffled down to the river, Weasel said, "You're a good human being, Striker. I always said so, stupid sometimes and hard-headed, but good in your heart. You'd make a good son."

Monahsetah was still sitting on the ground, coddling her bloody son. She didn't notice them until Striker spoke.

"Monahsetah. Look who I have found. He's a mess. Let me carry Yellow Bird across the water, and you let old Weasel lean on you. Maybe you could clean him up and stuff some weeds or something in his bullet holes, so he doesn't bleed all over me and my horse while we go to kill Custer."

An ancient crippled warrior rushed up, laid aside his spear, and took Yellow Bird as Striker came out of the river. "Help them, too," Striker said, nodding toward Monah-setah and Weasel, then ran to his tipi. Striker had ridden a captured cavalry mount back from the first fight south of camp, and left it with his mother. Now, as he remounted, Cranky Bear scolded him.

"Don't be in such a hurry to get killed. Haven't you fought enough? You'll get this fine big horse killed, too."

"I have to go, Mother. I'm a warrior, like

my father was."

"Your father was a fool, killed counting coup on a soldier with a gun. Anyhow, there are some cartridges in the horse pockets. I kept the other trinkets and food."

Striker reached back into the saddlebags. There were .45-70's, plenty of them, which might be handy if he captured a cavalry carbine, but there was also a nearly full box of .45 Colt pistol cartridges. "Weasel can use these. I'm going to carry him up to the fight."

"He's an old fool too. Did you know that your whore friend's child was killed?"

"She is not a whore, mother. And yes, I know. I carried him back across the river."

"Him? I'm talking about her." Cranky Bear Woman pointed to a small figure in yellow buckskin, face down in a pool of blood. "Did something happen to her half-white son too?"

Striker stared at the tiny body in momentary shock. The red and yellow were in sharp contrast with her black hair. *Like a butterfly,* he thought, then bent and grabbed his mother's braid. "Yes. She has lost both children. And this is no time for you to be mean. You clean up that little girl, and comfort Monahsetah when she comes, or I will come back and beat you with a stick."

Staggered by the change in her boy, she lowered her eyes and said, "Yes, my son."

As he turned to ride away he muttered, "Monahsetah's going to be really crazy now."

CHAPTER TWENTY

John Boye

"Gunfire is picking up to the north, Johnny. Custer must be into it now."

Color Sergeant Boye rubbed his face. "Both riders the Boy General sent said that he had 'em on the run. It sounds like it, don't it?"

Sergeant Daniel hawked and spat again. "I ain't sure how you knows just exactly who is running."

"Yeah. Well, once the pack train is here, I 'spect we'll take the ammunition and move up. Anyways, Major Reno is finally back in the perimeter."

"Where's he been?"

"Went back down to the river bank to try to get Lieutenant Hodgson's body, half-hour ago. Now Cap'n Weir wants to take D Company and ride to Custer, case he needs help."

As they watched, Major Reno shook his

head, denying Captain Weir's request. Weir shouted something at him, strode to his company, spoke to his executive officer, then rode north with only his orderly. Minutes later, his second-in-command saddled up D Company and they rode out to follow their commander.

Boye walked over to where Benteen and Reno stood. "Are we letting them go it alone, Colonel Benteen?"

Benteen turned to Reno. "What of it, Major? Custer said he wanted us to come, though he's probably finished 'em by now."

Reno took a sip from a hip flask. "I've got to wait for the pack train. Got to get a shovel so's we can bury poor Hodgson."

When Benteen fixed him with a cold stare, Reno continued lamely, "I'll send someone to follow Weir, and tell him to go ahead and find Custer. And we'll be along as soon as we have the ammunition packs. My men need to replenish, you know. Yours haven't even fired a shot yet."

Benteen snorted and walked away. As Boye caught up with him, Benteen said, "We'll take H, K, and M companies, and ride after D Company. Tell the sergeants to get 'em saddled. I'll brief the officers."

A lieutenant galloped past them, racing north to catch Captain Weir.

Striker

"I hope we get there before they're all wiped out," said Weasel. He had a death grip on Striker's shoulder, as Striker pushed the big horse up the side of Deep Coulee.

They passed groups of women who were stripping and mutilating the dead cavalrymen in the gully. The firing uphill ebbed and surged.

As they came to the top of Deep Coulee, they saw more of the battlefield sprawling before them. Bluecoats were in bunches, spread out much farther than a rifle could shoot. Most were fighting dismounted, though a larger group of a hundred or so could be seen through the smoke and dust riding over a knoll to the north. They were angling toward the third ford, at the north end of the village.

"Creeping Panther will be there," said Striker. "Most of the flags are there. I think he's trying to capture the women again, like he did at the Lodge Pole River, so we can't shoot at him."

Suddenly a large group of Bluecoats mounted and charged downhill toward them. Lakotas and Cheyenne scattered

178

before the charge but returned heavy fire. As the Bluecoats began to dismount and form a fighting line, Striker had a clear shot at one of their leaders, a tall man with stripes on his sleeves. His first shot hit the man's horse. When his smoke cleared from his second shot the wounded horse was bolting directly at him with the bloody-faced soldier clinging to its neck. As the crazed sorrel thundered past them downhill, Weasel fired several more pistol shots at the wounded man.

"I hit him," Weasel shouted, as dust flew from bullet strikes on the Bluecoat's body and leg. They watched as the runaway bore down on the river crossing, then veered left and raced up Medicine Tail Coulee and away from the fight. Shouting caused them to turn back to the fight just as more soldiers mounted and followed some other leaders to chase after the wounded man. Dozens of mounted warriors swarmed after them, and Striker started to join the chase but Weasel struck him on the side of his head with a pistol and said, "Hey — we're after Creeping Panther."

Far off to their right front, another Blue-coat suddenly mounted and rode through the Cheyenne surrounding his group, tear-ing away to the east. Several warriors wheeled and chased him, but his bigger grain-fed mount began to pull away from the grass-fed Indian ponies. Just as his young pursuers ran out of arrows and gave up the chase, the soldier shot himself in the head and tumbled from his horse.

"Aiieeyah," said Striker. "Did you see that?"

"Most Whites are very strange," said Weasel, "but I don't think he meant to do that. Maybe he was beating his horse with his pistol, and it went off. Look. You have a good shot here at those men he rode away from. They're too far for my pistol."

There were five or six troopers still firing from behind dead horses, sixty steps away. About twenty warriors were bobbing up and down in the deep grass around the soldiers, sending in a steady stream of bullets and arrows as they closed in.

Striker stood in the stirrups and put five quick rounds from his Winchester into the group.

"I think I hit one," Striker said straining to see through his own smoke. To his amazement, two of the troopers suddenly rose to their knees, placed their pistols against each other's heart, fired and fell over. A third soldier stood and fired two pistol shots at the surrounding Cheyenne, who had stopped their assault, apparently stunned by the suicides. Before they could react, the soldier then placed the Colt's barrel in his mouth and blew off the back of his head.

The last two badly wounded soldiers struggled to stand and tried to surrender. The Cheyenne quickly overran them and finished them with clubs and hatchets.

Striker kicked the horse into a gallop toward the last hill, as Weasel cheered and fought to hold on.

Monahsetah

Behind them, Monahsetah raced up Deep Coulee on foot, knife in hand, on her own mission. Between sobs, she screamed, "Both of them. Aiieeyah, both of them, and my father, too," until her throat was raw from the dust and smoke and yelling. On and on, like a deer, toward that smoky hilltop, more than a rifle shot away.

As she came out of the coulee she paused to catch her breath and was horrified to see that the soldiers with all the flags had disappeared over the hill. "Nooo," she screamed in frustration, "they cannot get away. It is not right!" She knelt, oblivious to the carnage around her, and hit herself on the sides of her head. "I waited for him," she sobbed. "Saved myself, even though he let his White wife send us away. Even though his men killed my father all those winters ago, I turned away many good warriors. Now he returns, not for me but to take the lives of my children? Oh, Ma'heo'o, how could you let him go? I wanted to see him dead!" Totally dejected, she finally stood and began to walk downhill, crying. Back to her dead babies. After many steps, she heard shouting and shooting behind her, and spun to see the Bluecoats ride back over the hilltop toward her, then stop and circle up as they were surrounded by warriors. "Oh yes," she said, and began running uphill again.

Striker

"Go right, Striker. Go over there, away from the river a little. We need to get around all these little bunches of fighters and get to that last hill. And we need to quit stopping for every little fight."

Striker grunted and took the big horse on a thundering run up a curving gully. As they popped out, they saw a civilian scout twenty steps away, back to them, kneeling among a cluster of dead soldiers and firing at some Lakotas across a deep ravine. Striker pulled up, and he and Weasel both fired as the man turned to face them. The bullets knocked him into the ditch formed by two dead troopers.

Striker rode closer, dismounted and tossed the scout's Yellowboy to Weasel, then undid the man's pistol belt. He had two Opentop Colts, and a belt full of .44 rimfires for them and the carbine. As he strapped on the pistols, he stared at the dead scout. He'd seen that face before, maybe long ago. *Penn? From Black Kettle's camp? No. Couldn't be.*

He pulled the saddle pockets from a nearby dead horse and rummaged through them, finding a small pistol and more cartridges, then slung the pockets over his horse's neck.

"You are a good human being, Striker, but slow. Do you not want to find Creeping Panther?" Weasel pulled Striker back up on the horse. "Maybe before dark?"

"Old man, you bark and whine like a toothless female dog. Look. I found you another pistol. Take it, and save your breath."

Weasel stuffed the little revolver into his parfleche, then wrapped his free arm around Striker's belly as Striker kicked the horse into a lumbering uphill run.

■ ■ ■ ■

Penn

As the Indians rode off uphill, the scout crawled up under one of the dead men, smeared blood on his face and head, and lay face down. "We'll just lie doggo here a bit," he muttered to himself. "Let 'em pass by, then grab some jerky and that little pistol out'n my saddlebags, and slip down to the river. Old Penn ain't finished just yet, not by a long shot."

Fifty steps downhill, several Cheyenne women had witnessed the brief fight, and now labored to get to the bodies. They carried knives, hatchets, and stone bone-marrow hammers. One long arrow flight behind them, Monahsetah still ran uphill. Her voice was gone.

Striker

As Striker and Weasel started up the last hill, the big horse took a bullet in the chest. He stumbled and went down. Just as Striker and Weasel jumped clear, a group of thirty or forty soldiers broke and ran away from them, downhill into a deep ravine.

Weasel yelled, "They're trying to make it to the river."

184

"Am I blind?" Striker snapped. "Stop telling me everything and shoot them."

Striker and Weasel emptied both carbines and all three Colts into the running soldiers, knelt to reload the carbines, then turned their attention back to the fight on the hilltop. As they began moving up again, a big Minneconjou Lakota named White Bull ran with them. "They killed my horse, too," he grumbled.

Still on the hill were about fifty soldiers, half down and half still fighting. Dead and wounded cavalry horses, perhaps thirty of them, were mixed with Indian ponies, flags, and hundreds of Lakotas and Cheyenne. The Indians dashed in to count coup, chop, shoot, take scalps, stab. Whinnies, screams of men and horses, gunfire, curses, smoke and dust filled the air.

Twenty steps from the top, a short-haired officer in a blood-stained blue shirt and white canvas pants pointed a Remington rifle at White Bull as he charged in, snapped on the empty chamber, then threw the rifle and reached for a pistol.

A few steps away, a second officer dressed completely in buckskins was on all fours, bleeding from the mouth and head, staring at the ground as they ran toward him.

"Custer," Striker shouted, in English. "Look at me!"

The kneeling man's head snapped up at the shout; he went to a sitting position and tried to pick up a small pistol.

"That's him!" yelled Striker. He fired, and Custer slumped over. Striker stood over him and fired three more rounds into his head before the Winchester ran dry. Weasel limped up and shot the dead man twice more.

Beside them, White Bull had counted coup on the other soldier by quirting him. The soldier snapped twice on empty chambers, dropped his pistol and began fighting with White Bull, punching and trying to bite his nose as they rolled on the ground.

"Hey, hey, come help me!" White Bull shouted, as he wrestled with the desperate tall man. Two other Lakotas swung their clubs but missed and hit White Bull instead. "You are not helping," he grunted. Weasel reached in with his knife and stabbed the soldier in the thigh, just as White Bull screamed in the man's face.

As White Bull broke free, the tall officer sat up and drew a second pistol, a short-barreled fat little five-shooter. Weasel drew the little pistol Striker had just given him and shot the soldier in the head. The man collapsed, dead as a stone. White Bull snatched the pistol from the dead soldier, hit him with it, then rushed away roaring, "Hoka Heyyy!"

Striker picked up a trooper's carbine and found it had an empty cartridge jammed in the chamber. He reversed it and, using the butt, began hitting the man in buckskin he had killed. After several blows, he realized that the shooting around them had stopped. The other warriors had grabbed the soldiers' weapons and rushed downhill to help finish the group of soldiers that had run toward the river.

"I think you have finished," said Weasel, sitting on the haunch of a dead horse. "His head is flat now, like buffalo droppings. Besides, you've been shot. And my leg hurts. Let's go tell Monahsetah."

CHAPTER TWENTY-ONE

Monahsetah

Monahsetah slowed to a fast walk as she approached the group of women below the last hill. They were singing and laughing. They had stripped six dead Whites and were starting the mutilations.

As a fat Cheyenne woman bent to cut off a bloody man's privates, he yelled, pushed away the knife and punched her. Monahsetah stopped to catch her breath. The wounded man jumped up and began a death dance with the fat woman, spinning, struggling to avoid her bite and her knife. As the woman cursed and screamed for help, her friends collapsed in laughter. On the second spin, Monahsetah recognized him. Penn.

In three steps Monahsetah was behind the naked man. She jammed the knife up under his ribs and he arched as she twisted. He squealed like a pig. The fat woman, suddenly pushing against nothing, fell to her hands and knees. Penn faced Monahsetah, scrabbling vainly for the thing in his back.

She thought she saw the recognition in his eyes, as he dropped to his knees.

He simply said, "You," and then his lights went out. He fell on his face.

As the women cheered, she put her foot in Penn's back, pulled out her knife and started uphill again. Her old friend Mahwissah joined her. Mahwissah was Black Kettle's sister, fellow slave of Creeping Panther, and his translator, all those years ago. All those memories came rushing back.

Mahwissah said, "Was that who I thought it was? Penn? The one who delivered you to Creeping Panther again and again? Is this Creeping Panther's force we are fighting? Again?"

"Yes," Monahsetah choked. "And they have killed my babies! I have to see him dead."

"Oh, little friend, and he's your husband. Oh, my heart breaks. I'll go with you."

John Boye

Three miles south of the smoky hilltop, Boye saw Captain Weir and his orderly pull up on a double-humped bluff, followed seconds later by Lieutenant Hare and Weir's

189

troopers. Ten minutes later, Benteen and Sergeant Boye joined them with Benteen's battalion. As the officers talked, Boye spoke to Sergeant Flanagan of D Company.

"Have you spotted the Boy General?" Boye grinned as he rode up. "He's gonna take a stick to these officers for not joining him sooner."

Flanagan's face was death-gray. "You better have a look-see, Johnny." He handed his telescope to Boye. "I think Custer's luck has finally run out."

The hills and ridgelines to the north were covered with mounted warriors and squaws on foot. Some of the riders were still firing down at objects on the ground, but the gunfire was only sporadic.

Boye handed back the scope and stared at Flanagan in shock. Flanagan nodded in confirmation and added, "The real firing stopped ten minutes ago, just as we rode up here. I think they're finishing the wounded now, and a lot of 'em is heading this way. That's a heap of damned Indians, Johnny. I think Custer's gone, and we're next. Jesus, that's over two hundred men dead. What've we got left?"

Boye looked at his timepiece. 5:35 PM. "Not enough. Maybe three-fifty. Depends on how many Reno lost in the valley."

Within minutes, the retreat to Reno Hill began, and hundreds upon hundreds of warriors started toward them.

Monahsetah

As Striker and Weasel limped downhill, dozens of women streamed around them, singing, stripping and cutting. They met Monahsetah and Mahwissah about half-way down.

"Did you find him?" Monahsetah rasped. "Is he dead? What happened to your head?"

Striker had a red plaid scarf wrapped around his head. It was blood-soaked.

Before he could speak, Weasel answered. "Someone shot off Striker's ear, but Striker killed Custer. I helped him, and then he mashed Custer's head."

"Show me," she said, pushing past them.

Groaning, they turned and followed her back up the hill.

Cheyenne and Lakota women were already stripping the two officers that Striker and White Bull had wiped out.

"That's him," Striker said dully. He pointed to the battered body of the man he'd killed. "You may not recognize him, but I called his name in his language and he looked at me. That's Custer."

"Yes, that is a Custer, but it is his brother

Tom. Those ink marks on his arm are called tattoos. This one over here is Creeping Panther. Get away from him!" Mahwissa hissed at a warrior, who was trying to cut off Creeping Panther's trigger finger. "He is kin."

Striker and Weasel stared at the man White Bull had fought with. Nude, except for a sock. Bullet holes in the temple and chest, and Weasel's gash in his thigh. Yellow-Hair, himself. Creeping Panther.

Monahsetah stared too. The beard was gone, the hair much shorter than she remembered, but this was Creeping Panther. The Boy General. He was propped, sitting, his back against two dead soldiers.

Mahwissah drew an awl from her pouch, took another from Monahsetah, then knelt and drove one into each of his ears. "Maybe you will listen better in the next life," she whispered. Then pulling an arrow from the ground, she forced it up into his member and added, "And you won't poke any more girls with this, will you?"

The other women clucked approval, and one asked, "Can we cut off his head and arms for you?"

Monahsetah faced them and wheezed, "No. And if anyone else touches him, I will find them and cut off their heads. And other parts."

Striker put his arm around her, and they started the long walk back to the river crossing. Weasel hobbled behind them, using his Yellowboy as a crutch. He said, "I know what we should do. Let's take your mother, Striker, and go back to the Lodge Pole River. I've never liked it up here. Creeping Panther's gone now. Let's go home."

Striker said, "Maybe we'll do that. Give that little pistol to Monahsetah. You killed Creeping Panther with it, and she should have it. It's big medicine. We'll find my dead horse as we walk back and take those saddle pockets. There's bullets in them and other things."

Monahsetah took the little pistol and examined it. She whispered, "This is a good size for me, and look at the markings on it. White man's mark for five, three times. Perhaps that is even more good medicine. And I don't want to be called Monahsetah anymore. Custer is dead. I will be Meotzi again."

Cheyenne Women

Behind them, the women set to their bloody work, with some grumbling. An old woman shook her fist at the backs of the foursome.

"Why do we have to listen to her? Who is she, some medicine woman I never met?"

"Shhh. Sort of. She was Creeping Panther's slave. She could make him do things. Got him to let a lot of us women go free after he caught us, long time ago," Fat Duck said, as she sawed on the flat-headed man's left wrist. "I wouldn't have known that was Creeping Panther or that this was his brother, if she hadn't told us. But all White men look alike to me."

"Yes," added Bluebird. "They called her Monahsetah, but her real name is Young Grass Who Shoots in the Spring. Meotzi."

Striker

As they approached the crossing, Meotzi veered left, then collapsed at a bloody patch on the ground. "His blood," she moaned. "My son. He died here." She picked up handfuls of the sticky soil, and rubbed her face with it. "Aieeyah, aieeyah."

Cranky Bear Woman slogged out of the river, and labored up the slight incline to where they stood.

Striker moved to cut her off. "Mother, if you say something stupid, I will knock you down." He put his hand out, finger against her chest.

She brushed it aside. "Stupid? I just came

194

to tell you and her that her boy is not dead. The bullet did not go in his head, just cut it bad and made him bleed and sleep a lot. I left him with our medicine man. Now who's stupid?"

CHAPTER TWENTY-TWO

John Boye

John Boye lay in a half-stupor, trying to decide whether a couple of gunshots or several trumpets blowing reveille had jolted him out of a deep sleep. It was still so dark he could barely make out the time.

"Two thirty, is it then? Sweet Jesus. And I was dreaming we was surrounded by screaming Sioux, and Custer was coming to save us, but he kept getting farther away." Boye rubbed his eyes and realized he was talking to his commander. "That's the way of dreams, ain't it, sir?"

Captain Benteen sat a few feet away. "Were the hostiles well-armed? Were we thirsty and tired? Not much of a dream, I'd say, Sergeant. Except the part about our leader coming to save us. No, he's left us just like he left Joel Elliott and those troopers on the Washita, eight years ago. Just like he left Major Reno and his men on their own, down in the valley yesterday." Benteen stood and stamped his feet to get the circulation started.

Boye sat up and stretched. "Well, sir, I don't think he's coming either. I don't think he can. I think he finally bit off more than a mouthful, and he's done. And we're next. And I wish you'd stay down, sir."

"Horse pebbles, Sergeant Boye. Our illustrious leader is somewhere down river with a batch of captured women and children, his horses and men watered and fed. Probably just having a second or third go at some darling Cheyenne girl. You do remember how he fancies them?" Benteen hacked and spat. "By now he's had that newsman Kellogg write the story of how he rode through the whole Sioux nation with just two hundred men."

Boye knew better than to argue with the old captain on this subject; he'd heard it for eight years. "Well, Colonel, the General has left us, whether he's dead or just off sporting. How do we get through this day, and how long must we hold out?"

"We have over three hundred men on a hilltop, with plenty of food and ammunition. If we can get some water, they'll never take us. Indians are not good against dug-in fighters. Reno should have stayed in those trees down there. I wish we were all down there now, in some shade and with water at our back. But we'll do fine here, at least until General Terry or Gibbons arrives. I'm going to make one more tour of the perimeter and then get some sleep. Been up all night."

As dawn broke John Boye could make out the whole position of what he thought of as Reno Hill. It was like a large rectangular frying pan, maybe three hundred and fifty yards wide and two hundred fifty deep, with the 'handle' of the pan sticking out from the wide part another two hundred fifty yards to the south. The whole thing laid out sort of north-south, and sort of parallel to the river which was downhill and more than five hundred yards west. Several large ravines led from Reno Hill down to the river, which meandered north toward the village.

It was a bare hilltop with a depression in the middle of the square 'pan.' The six other companies were formed around the lip of the square with horses, mules, ammunition, supplies, and the 'hospital' in the center. H Company was most exposed as they occupied the long 'handle.'

There were other hilltops around them, but they were too far away to permit the heathens to lob arrows into the cavalry position. Unfortunately, the heathens now had over two hundred .45-70 carbines, fresh from dead troopers, and plenty of cartridges, to add to their own substantial arsenal. The hostiles were able to sweep Reno Hill, the whole frying pan and handle, with gunfire. Only the depression provided any relief.

The day became a slow-moving nightmare. Crispy heat, vicious thirst, deadly incoming fire against any exposed troopers. And there were too many exposed troopers, especially in Benteen's own H Company. Sergeant Boye scuttled over to where H Company's executive officer lay.

"Lieutenant Gibson, we has to get some fortifications up. All the other companies did. We should have put them up last night."

"But Colonel Benteen said to let the men sleep. He said he didn't think the Indians would be back today."

Sergeant Boye took a deep breath. "And he was wrong, wasn't he? Wake him up and ask him what he thinks now, sir."

"But he said to let him sleep. He's really tired, Sergeant Boye. A bullet hit his boot heel an hour ago, and he barely stirred."

Boye grunted. "At this rate, he'll be well rested when we're overrun. And I'm thinking he won't like that."

Boye jogged to Benteen's position, bullets kicking dirt around him. He slid in beside the sleeping captain.

"Sir. SIR! You gots to wake up, Colonel. Things ain't good, and they's getting worse. And Lieutenant Gibson don't seem to be himself, exactly."

Benteen groaned and looked around. "Having a monkey and parrot time of it, is he? At least I see Doctor Porter has gotten some fly tents up for shading the wounded."

Boye said, "Yessir. But most of the wounded is from H Company, Colonel. The other companies took most all the boxes, ammunition and food crates and such, and they has some protection. And the Indians is crowding in, and I ain't seen Major Reno."

Benteen stood up, straightened his pistol belt and said, "Come with me."

Boye said, "Sweet Jaysus," and followed Benteen as he strolled to the pack train, near the center of the position. Benteen rounded up a dozen skulkers and ordered them to move everything possible to H Company's exposed ridge. Saddles, food crates, sacks of bacon, and empty ammunition boxes soon became breastworks for Benteen's company. Benteen left to find Reno.

He was soon back with a few reinforcements from M Company and some lightly wounded men from the hospital area.

Boye said, "It ain't good, Colonel. They's close enough to throw rocks at us. And they has, for a fact."

Benteen drew his pistol and shouted, "We've got to charge them, boys. Drive 'em back. Are you ready, then? Your lives depend on it. Follow me!"

He went over the edge and led a charge for a hundred yards down the gullies toward the river. The Sioux and Cheyenne fled before the screaming troopers. As they double-timed back up hill, Boye and another trooper dragged a wounded soldier between them. When they dropped him behind the barricades to catch their breath, the wounded man said, "They was hopping and jumping like circus people, wasn't they? We did good, huh? Did you see the Colonel? Ain't he something?"

Benteen was standing over him. "It was a good charge, son. We drove 'em off. I'm proud of you."

"Is that you, sir? I can't see good. My eyes is fogged." He was rolled in a blanket and carried to the hospital area.

Boye checked his watch. "Just after nine of the morning. I believe these boys would follow you into Hell's mouth, Colonel, even on a hot morning."

Benteen looked around. "I think they just did. Did you see me make that shot at the bottom, John Boye? I took that wounded boy's carbine and hit one of those running devils right in the spine. That'll teach 'em to spoil my nap. Listen now, Sergeant Boye. The First Sergeant's been wounded. You need to keep up with me. We must keep these boys going. Check on ammunition, then see if there's any water left and take it to the hospital."

At the depression serving as the hospital, John Boye distributed what little water he'd collected, then found the wounded trooper he'd helped uphill. The man was propped up, sitting against a dead horse.

"They can't do nothing for me, Sergeant Boye, but I can see better now. I ast 'em to let me sit up so's I can see the boys at work. I wants to thankee for not leaving me down there for them devils to cut me up. Thankee," he wheezed, "thankee much." He coughed once, then slumped over dead.

Boye took the man's revolver and cartridge belt and started back toward H Company, only to see Captain Benteen striding toward him. Bullets whizzed around him and kicked up dirt at his feet. Boye squatted at the edge of the depression to wait for him.

As Benteen stepped into the slight safety of the depression he said, "Come with me again. We've got to get Reno to get out of his hole and act. The hostiles are bunching on the north side. He's got to push 'em back, like we did."

Boye groaned and stood to follow his commander. "Colonel, do we have to spend so much time upright?"

Benteen turned to him and said, "When the bullet meant for me is cast, it'll find me. You cannot hide from death, Sergeant. Ah. There he is, where I left him. In his little hole, still with his suitemate, Captain Weir."

Boye said, "Yessir, but I thought Captain Weir couldn't stand Major Reno."

Benteen grinned. "He can't. But he loves the drink more than he hates Reno, and Reno has plenty. Stand here, but be ready to go over the side."

Boye watched as his captain walked over and stood above the other two officers, smiling at them as he talked. As he waited, Boye checked the cylinders on the two pistols.

Reno suddenly shouted, "Well, if you can see them, you order the charge!"

Captain Benteen stepped up to the highest point on the northern perimeter, drew his revolver and shouted, "Boys, we've got to charge them and drive them back. Now's the time. Give 'em hell. Hip, hip, here we go." And he went.

Boye said, "Ah, shite!" and ran to join him. Major Reno joined the charge, and almost every man in the four companies on the northern half of the position moved downhill firing. Boye found himself beside Sergeant Jim Daniel who was cursing as he banged away with his carbine, slipping and sliding down the rocky ravine.

"You seem upset, James, m'boy."

"And that I am, Sergeant Boye. Private Golden wouldn't budge. He's sitting back there sobbing."

"Well," said Boye, "he should be more afraid of you than these heathens." He holstered his first pistol, empty, and drew his second one.

The charge only went fifty yards before Reno called it off, but it was enough. As they slogged back uphill, Boye said, "Don't be too hard on Private Golden. Our own Lieutenant Gibson chose not to join us this morning in H Company's sortie. I stepped over him, going and coming."

Jim Bob Daniel frowned. "Aye, John Boye, but Golden ain't no officer, is he? I'll have to deal with him. See him there? Knees drawn up like a school girl? Jaysus."

As Daniel started toward the shirker, the dirt by Golden's head kicked up in a violent spray tinged with pink and he fell over dead. Sergeant Daniel put his hands on his hips as he stood over Golden's body. "Well, m'boy, some heathen crack shot has jist saved you from a terrible ass-chewing." Two more bullets whizzed by Daniel as he knelt and returned fire.

Boye glanced at his watch. Ten o'clock. He walked, upright, back to H Company. To no one in particular he said, "Can't hide from it." Somehow Benteen's words, which should have scared the bejesus out of him, brought him instead a certain comfort.

About noon, Captain Benteen stood in the middle of H Company's position and shouted, "It must be a hundred degrees, boys. We must have water. K Company just tried it down river of us, but no luck. Too many hostiles still in the woods there. I think we can get to the river down this gully we cleaned out earlier. If I can get some volunteers to make the dash, I'll put our four best shots up here to cover you. You'll take just pistols and canteens. Sergeant Mechling here has just made the trip without covering fire, and he gave me a sip. It's cold and delicious, boys. Who'll go?"

Mechling winked at John Boye and whispered, "Sip, my ass. He guzzled half my canteen."

Almost all the men volunteered, but Boye chose twenty men and went. He had a few wounded, but none killed. Several sorties were made, ending the water emergency, and after three that afternoon the hostile fire slackened. By four it ended and the greatest problem on Reno Hill was the stench of dead animals. And dead men.

Around five heavy smoke from the valley across the river added to their discomfort. Boye found his commander and asked, "What're they up to, sir?"

Benteen said, "Probably set fire to the grass to cover their movement. I hope it's a movement away from us."

They could barely make out the sun as it sank through the smoke, when suddenly the cloud lifted, providing the damndest sight Boye had ever seen. At the far side of the valley, over two miles away, a dark carpet crept south. Over half a mile wide and maybe three miles long. Indians on horseback. Horses pulling wounded warriors and tents on travois. More horses. Many more.

Someone said, "My God! Look what we've been standing off. That's got to be five thousand Indians and what, ten thousand horses? My God!"

Benteen said, "I'd say closer to twenty
thousand."

CHAPTER TWENTY-THREE

Dobey

The three men stood at the counter which served as a bar in the Fort Lincoln sutler's store. Three small jars, each half full of amber liquid, rested in front of them. The sutler left the bottle and moved several feet away.

Dobey took a sip of his and said, "Good Lord, John Boye, is this the best you soldiers can get up here?"

Boye grinned and said, "Afraid so, for us poor soldiers anyways. Officers, now, they seems to have pretty good whiskey, thanks to asshole sutlers like ol' Cheater James there. Us, now, we got to make do with busthead shite like this."

James grumbled, "My name ain't Cheater James, damn yore eyes, Sergeant Boye. And you knows it. My friends all call me Jim."

"All two of 'em?" Boye took a swallow, then wiped his mouth and beard with the back of his hand. "Tell you what, bird brain, you step a little closer so's I don't have to exert myself, and I'll break that beak of your'n again for you. And maybe I'll change your name to Flat-Nose James." He laid his Remington on the counter.

James muttered something and moved farther away.

Melton had sniffed the liquor and swirled it, and now drank some. He choked a little. "Busthead, my butt. Some of that stuff ain't so bad. This here is darker than mule piss, but not near as good." He stared daggers at the sutler and said, "You just shut up and stay away from us while we talk." Turning back to John Boye, Melton said, "Hickok sent word that Penn was back with the Seventh Cavalry, which is how come we're here. Is he around?"

Boye took another sip. "I'm afraid you've wasted a long trip. Penn is dead. He was up here, but he was with those five companies that Custer took with him. They was the ones as got wiped out."

Dobey said, "We heard on the way in that Custer's whole command was wiped out. Had us worried about you and Jim Daniel."

"Naw," said Boye. "We was both with the other seven companies back on Reno Hill, maybe four mile from where Custer wound up."

Dobey said, "He split his command?"

"He did indeed," said Boye, "but worse, he split it four ways. One company was back with the ammunition and supply train. Sent Captain Benteen with three companies off to the west, chasing ghosts. I was with them . . ."

Melton interrupted. "Now, sometimes you say Benteen's a colonel. Is this more of that 'bree-vet' stuff?"

Boye laughed. "It is. He's a captain, but we calls him 'Colonel' to his face, 'cause of his Yankee rank in the war. Anyways, as I was saying, Brevet Major General Custer, he then sends Brevet Colonel Reno across the river to charge this big-ass village with three companies. Told Reno he'd support him with the last five companies, but he must've decided to ride farther along this ridge line above the river, and hit the village in the middle, or the far side, or both. We don't know, and ain't no one left to tell the tale. See, it's kindly like what he did at the Washita."

Dobey said, "Yeah, but that was near seven hundred of you against a sleeping camp, with what, maybe a hundred-fifty fighters? What were you up against here?"

210

"Maybe six hundred of us, counting scouts and farriers and all, versus fifteen hundred, maybe two thousand Sioux and Cheyenne warriors. They was over five thousand people in that village. Some folks is already claiming it was worse odds, like four thousand fighters, but I'd say they had us three to one, and we was all split up. Until it was too late.

"Reno was s'posed to charge right through the village, but he pulled up short, then went in some woods along the river, then retreated and crossed the river again and wound up on that hill. Benteen figured out Custer had sent him away from the action, so he turned us back and we hooked up with Reno's outfit on the hill. Custer sent word for us to join him and bring the ammunition packs, so soon as they caught up we set out to do that. We didn't make it even half way to Custer's group afore we saw they was all down already, scattered over a mile or two of ridges.

"From looking at the bodies later on, Benteen said Custer must have split up again, sent two companies down to attack the village center. They either got chased away or was recalled, and then Custer tried to make a crossing at the far end of the village, but got pushed back up on higher ground, where he was finished off. And took two hundred good men with him. Except maybe one."

Melton's eyebrow went up. "You ain't gonna tell me you couldn't find Penn."

Boye said, "Naw. It took a while, with all of 'em cut up and naked and bloated. But I found Mister Penn, all right, leastways his head and hand and pecker, which was stuffed in his mouth. His hand was right beside the head and it was missing half the middle finger. He got it shot off in a fight down in New Mexico Territory. Used to stick that nub in his ear or nose as a joke. Looked like his whole finger was up into his brain or forehead or somewhere. It was him. They was a scar, too, along his cheekbone that we all knowed. I had several of the boys look to make certain sure I's right. I knew you'd want that, Boss Melton. He's gone. Right now wolves and buzzards is picking at his bones. Won't none of them boys buried deep."

It was quiet for a while as they sipped the bad whiskey. Finally Dobey said, "Well, who got away? A friend?"

"Not exactly, but I knew him. Sergeant Frank Finkle was the tallest man in the regiment. We found his friend Sergeant Finley and some more C Company boys in a skirmish line down toward the river. Then we found Sergeant Butler and Corporal Foley, another C Company man, a half mile or better back to the east like maybe they made a run for it. Just here last week they found another dead C Company man, Private Nathan Short, twenny-five miles east of the fight over on Rosebud Creek, him and his horse on top of him. Never found Lieutenant Harrington's body neither, but we figure Tom Custer musta left him in charge of his C Company, since Tom was found with his brother on Last Stand Hill.

"Then we found a dead C Company sorrel maybe eighty miles east and north, clean up to the Yellowstone. Four white stockings on the carcass like what Sergeant Finkle rode, shot in the head and a carbine laying by it, but never found the Bean Pole's body. It shoulda been there, or on the battlefield, and it woulda stood out.

"Don't say I told you, but the body count don't add up. We're missing maybe five or ten troopers. Hard to say exact, seeing as they was cut up so bad, but could be that many. I figure Lieutenant Harrington and Bean Pole Finkle led a C Company breakout run back east and kept going until they was run down or got away. The Crows says they's found another five or six dead soldiers in a circle miles east of the fight, sort of a second Last Stand. Anyhow, because of that lone dead horse I keep hoping Finkle'll show up."

"Thought you said he weren't exactly a friend," Melton said.

"He ain't, but he owes me five dollars. Anyways, after they finished Custer, all them hostiles come after us. We skedaddled back to Reno Hill and held them off that night and the next day, and then they pulled up stakes and left. And the next day the relief column found us. Benteen wouldn't believe Custer was dead at first. Still figured he'd left us like he left Elliott back in '68. I mean everybody knew about Custer's Luck and how he always squeezed out of a tight spot. Well, General Terry ordered Benteen to take H Company to Custer Hill to see for hisself. I'm with him. Custer was laying buck naked against some other bodies, almost sitting up, not cut up too bad. Ears was punctured, bullet holes in his head and chest, a cut in his thigh, trigger finger near sawed off, and a arrow up his pecker. Looked right peaceful."

"Not cut up too bad, did you say? Jesus!" Melton snorted.

"Jaysus, yourself. You shoulda seen the others. Only way we picked out Lieutenant

Crittenden was an Indian had shot an arrow right into his glass eye. Shattered it, but leastways we could tell it was him. Never found Lieutenant Sturgis' body, but we think his head was one of several in a fire pit in the village. He was Colonel Sturgis' boy."

Dobey said, "So, who's Sturgis?"

"He's a real colonel, and he's the real commander of the regiment. Been on 'detached duty' almost forever. Sitting in some office back east. Custer, being only a lieutenant colonel for real, he was the Executive Officer and the Acting Commander."

"For like nine years." Melton snorted again. "And y'all thought he was lucky?"

John Boye looked pained. "He was, Boss. It's a wonder he weren't killed a dozen times. Back in Kansas in '67, he took out alone across the prairie with his dogs, got way ahead of the regiment, maybe five miles, and us hunting Indians. He come up on a lone buffalo bull and decided to try and kill it with his pistol. A pistol, mind you. Well, the bull turned into his horse, Custer grabbed the reins with both hands and shot his own horse in the brain pan. He jumped clear and the bull stopped and turned on him. Hell, that bull shoulda finished him right then and there. That's what woulda happened to you nor me, but Hell no, not Custer. This pissed off old bull just stares at Custer a minute or so and then just strolled away. Anyways, there's our fearless leader with just his dogs and a pistol, miles from nowhere. Does his gunshot bring a party of Cheyenne Dogmen to polish him off, out there all alone? No, Hell no. Scouts finally found him, though he hid from 'em for a while thinking they was hostiles, and then they had to go back a couple miles to get his saddle. Ever' time he got in hot water, that famous Custer Luck got him out. 'Cept this once."

Melton downed his whiskey and grimaced. "By God, I wanted Penn myself, but if you're sure he's gone, I guess our work's done up here. You ready to start back, Dobey?"

"Yeah, we better. We'll go ahead and stock up for the trip, but I thought we'd swing by Deadwood and see Hickok on our way south." Dobey pushed the last of his drink away and slapped a coin on the bar.

Boye finished his jar and said, "That's a lot of open plains 'tween here and Deadwood. You want a small cavalry escort?"

Melton said, "Hell yes, we do!"

Dobey said, "You serious?"

Boye grinned. "I said small and I meant

it. It'd be me. My times 'bout up, and if you can wait a few days I'd like to ride with you. I hate it up here."

Dobey said, "What about your pension? No way you got enough time in yet."

Boye shook his head. "Nope. But I still got most of that Pinkerton money that me and Walter Kennedy collected when them Pinkertons wouldn't wait for an escort. You recollect?"

Dobey nodded. Pinkertons chasing him and Melton had approached Sergeant Boye in Fort Dodge back in '68, and he'd sent them off the wrong way toward Abilene. They'd refused to wait for an escort and set out with two hired guards. A patrol had found them the next day forty miles east, shot full of arrows. Their reward money, over one thousand in paper bills, had been stuffed in their mouths or was blowing in nearby bushes. John Boye and his boss, Sergeant-Major Walter Kennedy, had collected it all from the troopers who recovered it, declaring it was "evidence." And then Kennedy had been killed in the attack on Black Kettle's camp.

"It's grown some in eight years," Boye continued. "Ran some laundry operations, loaned a little out here and there. But I can always sign up again with one of them regi-

217

ments down south, if I start longing for poor pay, short rations, and hard times again."

Melton said, "Cap'n, let's wait for him. I felt near naked on the way up here, just you and me and Bear and Shelly. Couple more guns might help. Sure couldn't be no worse."

Dobey nodded. "All right. We'd like that, John Boye. Might be we can get Hickok to come back with us too, if he ain't been drawing too many aces down there in Deadwood."

CHAPTER TWENTY-FOUR

Meotzi

"We need to just leave her and her sick boy somewhere and move faster. You are such a stupid son. Can't you see that?" Cranky Bear Woman clucked and swatted her horse again, causing the old mare to leap for-warded again, whereupon the old woman yanked back on the rope to slow down. Again.

Striker said, "Mother, we are not . . ."

Meotzi interrupted him. "You can talk to me, Old Woman. I'm right here. I don't need your spineless son to interpret your chatter."

Striker tried again. "Listen, you two, we need to . . ."

Cranky Bear Woman shouted, "Stop tak-ing her side on everything. I'm your mother. I'm old and have much experience in life. This woman," she pointed to Meotzi, "was married to that Creeping Panther soldier devil, and now we've killed him and many of his men. And the other Bluecoats will come and wipe us out if we don't get far away. All the boy wants to do is sleep anyway. I think that Bluecoat bullet to his head has given him the sleeping sickness. He's probably dying."

Weasel said, "That is no way to talk. The boy is hurt and needs rest, but the bullet didn't break his head bone. He'll be fine . . ."

"Oh, so you're going to take up for them too, you old dog. You like me just fine when we share the blanket at night, but you have to strut like a turkey in front of this young woman? See how well you sleep tonight!"

The five weary travelers were riding through rough country, heading away from the great fight in the valley of the Greasy Grass, keeping the rising sun on their left.

"Mother we've come a long way. It's been over this many nights," Striker held up both hands, "but we can't go faster, not while pulling the travois with all our things. And if we left it all, the boy still can't ride fast and hard anyway. He is hurt."

Meotzi turned to stare into Cranky Bear Woman's eyes. "Why don't you ride on alone, you old hag? If you're afraid now, try that for a few days."

Cranky Bear Woman tossed her head. "I won't have to go alone. My warrior son will take me. You can keep the old one since he doesn't seem to care for my comfort anymore."

Weasel said, "I didn't say that. I just . . ."

"I'm not leaving Meotzi and Yellow Bird, Mother, so you better be nice to old Weasel if you really want to press ahead."

"I don't want to go on alone. But if we have to keep stopping for the boy to sleep, we'll never get back to the Lodge Pole River. Why don't we put him on the travois and just let him sleep all the time? At least then we won't have to stop so many times every day."

Yellow Bird halted his pony and stared straight at the sun. "Mother, it's getting dark very early today." He turned to smile at her, then pitched head first off the little paint.

"He has hurt his head again, Meotzi. That's a lot of blood."

"Am I blind, Striker?" She tied off the cloth bandage and stood. "Your mother finally had a good idea. We'll let him ride on the travois for a few days. One of you men ride on ahead and find a good place by some water for us to camp tonight."

Striker nodded, then mounted and rode

away through a cut in the hills, keeping the afternoon sun on his right.

Weasel

Cranky Bear Woman yelled over her shoulder, "We'll ride out a little, keep an eye on Striker's tracks, Meotzi. You just pull that travois as fast as you can and keep an eye on us. It was a good thought I had, to let your boy ride back there. Now he can sleep all he wants." She turned to Weasel and whispered, "Till he dies."

Weasel gave her a pained look and said, "But he's not dying, not for sure. I've seen many warriors hurt in their heads like this, and they act tired and crazy for a while and then many get better. Your husband didn't get better, but he was shot bad. He never had a chance."

"That's for sure," she muttered.

"Well, you tried. At least we got him home to you before he passed on. And our men killed the soldier who shot him."

She stared at Weasel so hard that he had to look away.

"I'm sorry," he mumbled. "I know it's hard for you, even after so long. And I've always felt bad that we laid together before he was killed."

"Before he was killed? You mean, while he

222

was being killed, don't you? You old fool, you don't know what you mean and you don't know much. That little boy is going to get us all killed, and for what? He's dying anyhow. Next time his mother goes in the bushes, or tonight while she sleeps, you put your hand over her boy's mouth and nose and he'll be out of his pain. And we can start moving. You do it, or I will."

Weasel stared at her. "You could not do such a thing. I know I could not."

She stared back. "Do you think my husband died on his own? He was like this boy, dribbling, drooling, wetting himself. I hated him. He used me rough, and he treated Striker like a dog before he was shot. I was glad the soldier shot him. I just wish he was a better shot, and I didn't have to finish it."

Weasel was speechless.

She started on him again. "Why didn't you marry me? You know he was a mean man. You should have taken me away from him, but even after he was dead, you didn't marry me. You left me alone, until now."

Weasel said, "I felt so wrong. I was happy when he rode away on that war party. I should have gone too, but I played sick so I could sleep with you for three or four days. And Striker was too small to bother us. And since your husband died, you've acted like

223

you hated me."

"I do hate you! I've had no man to take care of me, all this time, except my son. And all I ever wanted was you."

He said, "I don't think you know how your bitterness drives people away. Drives me away, anyhow. It's like bad fruit."

She said, "And you don't know why I'm bitter? I would have killed myself, years ago, but I had to raise Striker. My son. Our son, you cracked-head old fool."

Weasel felt like an axe really had been buried in his head. "You, you . . . This is really . . ." he fumbled. "You just stay away from that little boy." He dropped back to ride beside Meotzi.

"What's wrong with her?" Meotzi asked.

He shook his head, "Everything."

Striker

By the time the sun had fallen half-way back to the ground Striker had crossed two low ranges of hills and then he found what he sought; good clear water coming down from one of the big mountains. The stream ran alongside a rocky outcrop with a large ledge which was surrounded by a dense thicket of alder and cottonwoods. He let his horse drink, then tied it off by the ledge. He traded the positions of his weapons, taking his bow in hand and slinging his carbine across his back.

Upstream, not even a rifle shot distant from the campsite, he put an arrow through the shoulder of a fat doe as she drank from the noisy creek. She bolted, of course, but he soon found her and cut her throat. The deer was too fat to carry so he walked back to get his horse to bring the carcass to camp.

As he walked the pony along the creek to the kill site, he thought, *This is good. I can dress it, and start a fire under the ledge, and hang the meat so it smokes some before I get back with the others. And we can bathe in the stream. Maybe I can see Meotzi without her clothes once more.*

Lost in thought, he came into the little clearing where he'd left the dead deer and found her again — but with a man standing over her. The man held a Spencer carbine ready, but not pointed at Striker. Striker could not tell if he was white or Indian; he wore deerskin clothes, a flop hat and moccasins, and was dark skinned. His face was like leather, and he wore no face hair.

The stranger gave the peace sign, then said white words.

"Your kill? You parlay English some, maybe?"

Striker, wired tight but with his Winchester

225

still across his back, felt a deep sense of relief as he sensed no hostility or greed or fear in the white man.

"My kill," he said. "No much White talk. Can some, but no much. Sign, can do."

The white man said, "I sign. Have to, living out here and trading with Injins regular. I'll help you dress your deer. Trade you for the skin. My name is Isaac."

Striker, using a few words and a lot of sign, told Isaac that he'd like to share the meat, but he had to feed his 'family' of three more adults and a hurt child. Then he said, "You take skin. No worry."

Isaac said, "Hell, I got plenty food. Tell you what, you go bring your people to my cabin. I'll feed you and I got some medicines too. It's on upstream a piece, on t'other side. I'll dress your deer out, and get her on the fire too. Bring that child and I'll take a look and see can I help."

Striker felt funny about leaving his kill with the stranger, and yet it was good somehow. It hit him, halfway back to the others. The man was like those men at Balliett's Post, all those years ago. Someone you could trade, smoke, and talk with — and laugh. Easy enough to steal from, or even kill, but you didn't need or want to.

When he explained it to Weasel that way,

the women wailed and said he was crazy.

Weasel said, "I understand. You women shut up. We're going there. This is good. And if Striker is wrong and the man wants to take his deer, we'll kill him and take everything he has. Except those sock things they wear. They smell bad."

CHAPTER TWENTY-FIVE

Dobey

"So we gonna catch this boat to get us over the river? Like a ferry?" Bear was eager to head home to Canadian Fort.

Dobey said, "Well, if we were gonna go cross country, that's what we'd do. John Boye's talked me into another plan. We're gonna load the horses on a river steamer, go down the Missouri to the Cheyenne River, then up it far as we can towards Deadwood."

John Boye said, "Save us a bunch of riding, and time. And danger. You been on a riverboat before, Bear?"

"Couple of 'em, Sergeant Boye. Back when me and Mama and Honey first met Boss Melton and The Cap'n. Shelly ain't never done it though."

Boye smiled. "Well, Miz Shelly, I'm thinking you'll find it's a fine way to travel."

Shelly nodded, but pointed at a man wearing black wool clothing, despite the July Dakota heat. "Why does he wear his shirt backwards?"

"Man of the cloth," Boye said, frowning. He spat.

"Priest of some sort," said Dobey. "It's how they dress."

"Might be Catholic or Epistithalian," said Melton. "We seen a Catholic one in South Carolina, outside Columbia. Stopped him 'cause he was riding towards the coast and looked like he'd been fighting. Said he stood up from sitting on a toilet, hit his head and had to bandage it. Ain't ever seen the other kind, but Dobey says they's sorta the same."

Everyone stared at the skinny priest for a moment. Shelly asked, "What's a toilet?"

Melton shrugged. "Hell, child, I don't know. I ain't Catholic."

Fifty miles downstream, Dobey happened on John Boye in the livestock section of the boat. Boye was intent on the priest, who was brushing down an old mule.

"Easy to see you don't cotton to him," said Dobey. "You know him?"

"Not him, exactly, but maybe one like him," Boye replied.

Dobey waited, and finally Boye continued. "We're Irish, you know, so's we went to

Catholic school. There was one priest tried to lay hands on me. Me older brother, Padraig, he'd warned me, so I pushed him away and said I wasn't like that."

"That's it?"

"No, that ain't all of it. The good Father had some older boys hold me, pulled down my drawers and caned me good. When I told my Dad he beat me too, and my Ma carried on at me like a banshee. Told my brother, and he got drunk. So I run. Got work on a horse farm and soon's the war come I joined the cavalry. And if I see him," Boye jabbed a finger toward the priest, "even look sideways at some wee boy, I will throw him off this boat. And maybe gut him first."

Dobey said, "I s'pose you've noticed there are no wee boys on this boat."

"All the same," Boye almost shouted. "It's all of a piece. He'll slip, faith be with us, and I'll have him." He slapped a stall wall, startling a pony.

The priest looked at them, put away the brush, and wiped his hands on his shabby robe as he walked over to them.

"Faith, and I heard a sliver of the old country just then. Music to my ears. Would ye both be from Ireland then?" He stuck out a hand.

Dobey shook his head but Boye swatted the hand away. "And what brings you out here, Father? Looking to set up a school for boys?"

The priest looked confused "I was, in fact. But Fort Lincoln had a good school, and with the troubles to westward, I thought I'd try Fort Pierre."

Boye's nostrils flared. "Someday, one of those boys will kill you. What did I tell you, Dobey? What did I say?" Boye stormed off.

The priest turned to Dobey, palms up. "Does he think he knows me? I don't think I know him, so I don't know how I offended him."

Dobey shrugged and stared at the man. "Somebody like you, maybe?"

"And I must answer for someone else's sins," the priest said, turning away. "God save me. Once again it happens."

CHAPTER TWENTY-SIX

Meotzi

"I can talk some more white words than these two fighters, and my son can talk some too. Maybe not so good because I have been away from my husband's people for many summers. It will come back to me maybe some if you talk with me." Meotzi signed as she spoke, and the white man nodded to show he understood her. It surprised her, and made her feel good.

"What about the old woman? She parlay any English? White, I mean?" The trader flicked his eyes toward Cranky Bear Woman as he spoke.

"Her? She no can say shit in white talk. Not even." Seventh Cavalry troopers had taught Meotzi most of her limited white talk, and she was proud of it. "No more little talk. You have white medicines? Can help Yellow Bird yes?"

Isaac nodded again. "I do. Mebbe I can.

Got a powder to put on that cut but first-off we'll splash some liquor on it. A blue coat doctor tole me that can help. It appears to me as if he has a concussion."

"What that is?" Meotzi frowned, and shrugged an "I don't know" look back at her traveling companions.

"Means I think his brain has been knocked loose from his brain-pan. Needs to rest, sleep a lot and let it grow back together, sort of. Y'all can lay over here. I got plenty food, and I like company."

"Company? What company? You mean Horse Soldiers?"

"No, no, no. I mean 'friends,' like you-all." Isaac hugged himself. "And you-all are Shahiyena, right? Cheyenne. Not Lakota?"

"We are Tsitsitas. The People. Lakota call us Shahiyena. Those Who Talk Different. You Whites say Cheyenne."

Cranky Bear Woman turned to Striker and asked in Cheyenne, "Is she making fun of us?"

Striker said, "I don't think so."

"I think we should just kill him and take what we need and move on. Or leave her and the boy and steal what we need while they sleep."

Weasel pinched her shoulder. "Be silent, old woman. This man is a good one. Don't

233

you think so, my son?"

Striker grimaced. "It makes me crazy to think of you as my father. But I think you are right."

CHAPTER TWENTY-SEVEN

Dobey

Dobey, Melton, and John Boye were leaning on the bow rail, enjoying the fast downriver run toward Fort Pierre when the Quartermaster approached them.

"You folks doing all right?" He cupped his hands to fire up a cigar. "I mean, no problems with our smoky old boat?"

Dobey said, "Sure beats going cross-country, 'specially in this heat."

"Faster, too," said Melton.

"Told you so," said Boye.

"Yep. River behind us, a-pushing us along, we can purt' near fly. Now, somebody said y'all was heading for Fort Pierre, and another person thought it was Deadwood. Which is it?"

"Faith," said Boye, "I think it's both. Something wrong with my plan?"

"No," said the Quartermaster, "but they is two ways to skin that cat. You could go to

Fort Pierre, then hook up with one of the wagon trains a-going in to Deadwood. That's the slow way. But the Cheyenne River peels off this here Missoura River maybe sixty, seventy miles this side of Fort Pierre. Heads due west, right towards Deadwood. A flat bottom boat, like this'n, it could get you maybe another forty miles closer to Deadwood. I mean, if'n you could get one."

"How would a body do that?" asked Dobey. "Get a boat like this, I mean. Do we just get off at the Cheyenne River and head west, hoping a boat comes along?"

"You could do that. That's prob'ly the cheap way." The Quartermaster winked. "Or you could slip me a few dollars to grease the skids with the Captain, see would he take a two day side trip. He'd want extry pay, for the fuel and all, of course."

Dobey said, "Five dollars enough to get this started?"

"More'n enough," the man grinned. "But I'll take it."

The Quartermaster touched his cap brim and headed up the steps toward the wheel-house.

Boye said, "Well, while he's greasing skids or palms or whatsomever he does, I'm gonna go see what I can learn about the country between us and Deadwood. They is one or two scouts on board."

As Boye walked off in one direction, the priest approached Dobey and Melton from the other.

"Has your friend figured out that he doesn't know me?"

Dobey said, "Padre, I don't think it matters. I tried to tell you, it's your type he doesn't care for."

The priest shook his head and stood silent for a moment. He was taller than Melton, but raw-boned and not as heavy. Anywhere from thirty-five to fifty years, thought Dobey. With that leather face and those sad eyes, who could tell?

The man looked down at Dobey and spoke with a sudden urgency that startled both Texans. "I should let it go, but I can't. It's too important. To me, anyway. I can only guess what happened to him to make him so hostile, but he's wrong."

"Yeah, and just how do we know that?" said Melton.

"He's wrong about me and about most priests," the man insisted. "A few bad apples give many good men of God a bad name. I take it especially hard because it was such behavior that got me defrocked."

"Say what?" said Melton. "De-what?"

237

Dobey said, "Defrocked. Kicked out of his religious order. But you said you weren't like that."

The man sighed. "It wasn't my behavior, at least not along those lines. I had already gotten in trouble for shaking a father — a parent, that is — who was caning his young son. Then I caught an old priest molesting a boy in our congregation, back in Saint Louis, and I beat him."

"You beat an old priest?"

"I used to have a problem with my temper. I beat him badly. Broke his jaw. He had made an advance to me some time earlier, and I had warned him." The man shrugged. "I couldn't control myself and I'm ashamed, but it's done. They gave me the boot."

Dobey said, "And so you've joined another order?"

"No, and I have not. I'm sort of black-listed, d'ye see. No longer Father O'Hanley, I'm just Mike O'Hanley now. But I'm a damned fine teacher and disciplinarian, even without a cane, and I don't know anything else. So — I travel about, wearing these hot robes, teaching wherever there's need and money or food."

Melton said, "Why in the hell wear the robes, then?"

"Helps to get work. Except when I run

238

into some poor wronged soul like your friend John Boye."

Dobey said, "Would you preach, if some town gave you a church?"

"In the flick of an eye, I would. In my mind I'm still a priest. I've done it and I'd do it again, until I'm uncovered by the Holy Catholic Church. That's why I've come so far west, but your frontier is a double-edged sword for me. D'ye see, there are many communities out here that need a church but the reason they don't have one is they don't want one."

Dobey nodded. "Then, as civilization advances, so does Mother Church. And you have to move again."

O'Hanley smiled. "Just so."

Melton said, "Lemme ask you one thing. If you ain't fond of boys, how come you give up women?"

"And that's been the hardest part for me, 'cause I did give them up," said O'Hanley. "It's not like I never knew that pleasure. I wasn't young when I got my calling. I fought in Mexico as a boy back in forty-eight. That's where I got this." He pulled up his robe to show them a deformed calf, missing much of the muscle. "Grapeshot. Mustered me out, it did, and in three years I was a full-blown drunk back in South

Boston. I sobered up in prison after I crippled a man in a fight over a woman. And here I am."

"I got one more question," said Melton. "What's a frock?"

John Boye

"Well, you may take his pap and swallow it if you so chooses. As for me, I'm thinking he's had years to polish that story. He's so much as told you he's a fraud." John Boye spat, then gave Dobey a defiant stare.

"If he's lying, he's pretty good. He convinced me," Dobey said. "Melton too. We even talked about asking him to come home with us. Maybe start us a school."

The two men were exercising their horses ashore while providing some security for the beached riverboat which was taking on firewood from a heavily wooded patch along the east bank. They were riding almost a mile northeast of the boat, while Bear and Melton were out a similar distance to the southeast.

"Soon as we're back on board, I'm gonna have a talk with him my own self. See if he can convince me," said Boye. "You might not want him near your young ones."

"I got a good view from this hill. I can handle this side alone. You go on back and have your little talk." Dobey waved to the expansive view, then added, "You just make sure they bang off a round to tell me when to come in."

On the riverboat, John Boye paid a stable hand a dime to strip his tack and rub down his horse, then went looking for the false priest O'Hanley. He soon spotted his quarry on the lower deck, walking away toward the stern. Boye quickstepped to catch him, but before he was close, a woman turned the corner toward them and yelled over her shoulder, "Just leave me alone!"

Two men turned the corner behind her, pursuing her. Boye judged them to be a gambler and a miner from their clothes. The miner tripped the woman and as she scrambled back to her feet, each man grabbed an arm and pushed her against the railing.

"You giving it up to a nigger, you can give it up to us as well," the gambler said.

"No!" she said, and Boye recognized her. Shelly. Before he could yell, the priest was on them. He grabbed the miner's wrist, twisted it loose from Shelly's right arm and slammed the man back against the bulk-head, then stuck a big, boney finger in the gambler's face and said, "Let her go."

The gambler backed away and said, "Stay out of this, Padre. She's a Injun whore and she's taken up with some nigger buck. We mean to pay her, but she's just trying to hold out for more . . ."

"You meddlesome son of a bitch, I'll cut you from neck to nuts," yelled the miner, waving a giant Bowie and swaying on his feet.

O'Hanley swatted the knife hand away with his left and delivered a bone crunching right to the miner's face. The man dropped his knife, back-pedalled two steps, and sat down, his nose at a funny angle and bleeding. He touched his nose and fell over, out cold.

O'Hanley eased Shelly behind him with his left hand, and squared off with the gambler. "This lass is not interested in your attention. Touch her again and I'll hurt you. And you should probably go ashore and run before her husband comes back and learns of this."

"I ain't scared of no nigger nor no priest," the man said, as he drew a nickel-plated Remington. Before he could present it, he heard the four clicks of a Colt being cocked, and looked past the priest to stare into the muzzle of John Boye's .45.

"Step aside, Padre," Boye said. "I got this one."

O'Hanley moved the wrong way, putting

himself against the rail between Shelley and John Boye. The move blocked Boye's view for an instant and the gambler grabbed Shelly again, yanking her in front of him.

"Don't do anything stupid, laddie," said Boye.

"I'll leave, but I'm taking her with me. A hostage. I need horses saddled and brought up. Anybody tails me, I'll kill her. Be sure and tell the nigger I said so. And somebody go get my traps from my cot."

"I'll do that," O'Hanley said. At that moment, someone in the shore party fired a rifle to signal the end of firewood detail.

When the gambler glanced away, Boye shot him in the head. The shiny pistol clattered to the deck as the man collapsed like an empty suit.

Boye grabbed Shelley's arm and pulled the stunned woman to him. "Funny thing about a bullet through the brain-pan," he said. "A man don't stagger around much. Be a good lass now, and grab us that fine little pistol. I'm thinking the Father here might need it. And I'll have that large lovely knife me own self."

Boye, Dobey, and Melton met with the riverboat captain later that day as they approached the mouth of the Cheyenne River.

Standing on the foredeck, the captain spoke first. "John Boye, I know I told you I had reservations about trying to take y'all up the Cheyenne. First off, I don't know how far up it I can get you. Three mile? Twenty, maybe? Ain't no telling, even with all this late rainwater. Mainly though I was thinking y'all would be a lot safer going on to Fort Pierre and waiting for an ox train heading into Deadwood. Now I don't know."

Boye said, "And why's that? What's new?"

"I got that cross-eyed little trouble-maker locked up to keep your boy Bear from hurting him worse. Hell, that preacher done knocked his nose even more crooked than it were, and he might be even more cock-eyed. Says his name is Southerland, but others say he's Crook-Nose Jack McCall out of Deadwood. Him and that dead gambler been running a con with cards all the way down from Bismarck."

Dobey said, "What's all that got to do with us?"

"Sorry," said the captain. "I do tend to ramble. Thing is, this McCall kid has friends in Fort Pierre and Deadwood. Says the dead gambler was sent to Bismarck to get him to come back to Deadwood for some important job. Something to do with an election.

Says he's gonna get y'all arrested in Fort Pierre for murder."

"No way that charge could stick," snorted Melton.

"You don't know the courts out here. Even if it don't stick, they could hold you up for months for the trial. And there ain't no law in Deadwood, 'cept his friends. Damn gamblers."

"So what're you saying — you gonna put us off here?" Boye was starting to get hot.

"No. I'm saying y'all should probably do what you was wanting in the first place. I'll take you as far up the Cheyenne as I can and y'all go cross country fast as you can from there. I'll keep McCall in chains all the way to the Fort, and see can I tie him up there with the law. But even if they cut him loose right away, he'll be coming with a slow-assed ox train. Y'all can get there, do your business and get out afore he comes and muddies the water, so to speak, legal-like."

Boye said, "That laddie was so drunk, he's liable to wake up tomorrow and not even remember anything that happened."

Dobey said, "I think we'll take the Captain's advice. You got a handle on how to get there, John Boye?"

"I do, Dobey. North shore of the Cheyenne 'til it turns south where the Belle Fourche River runs into it, then follow the Belle Fourche to Bear Butte. It's some big-assed mountain we can't miss, then turn south on Bear Butte Creek and that sort of takes us in. Better'n all that though, I got a muleskinner who wants to go with us."

"A damn wagon?" said Melton.

"Yes, which we can sleep under. And four mules so he won't slow us much. He's going on past Bear Butte a day or so, dropping off supplies and picking up pelts and then back to Deadwood. Says he'll feed us if we let him ride with us. And do that extry leg with him, too."

Dobey said, "I don't know. Where's that extra leg to? And is he armed?"

"Got his grown boy with him, and they both got Winchesters and shotguns and two pistols. The far point is some little trading post. Name of Isaac's Store."

"I can't go no farther, Dobey. We're scraping bottom now. I got to back-paddle a half mile to that last bend to even turn around, but I can drop y'all off there." The Captain shouted some orders and the boat chugged to a halt, then slowly reversed.

"Thanks, Captain. I'll go get my gang ready. What do I owe you?"

"That dead gambler had some money on him. This side trip is his fault. We'll call it even. Listen now — you get to Deadwood, look up my old friend Bill Massie. We worked on these boats together for years. Tell him his friend Cap'n Cletus Williams gives his regards. Cap'n Bill Massie. He got the gold fever, left his boat, and is into land speculation, I hear. And gambling. If he ain't been shot yet."

CHAPTER TWENTY-EIGHT

Meotzi

Meotzi woke to the smell of coffee and bacon. She touched her son's face without waking him and was glad to find no fever. They were sharing Isaac's bed. The trader had insisted on it and had slept on the floor in the main room of his store. Striker and Weasel chose to stay outside.

She sat up, stretched, and became aware of sounds. Birds making morning songs, bacon sizzling in the other room, Cranky Bear Woman snoring on a robe on the floor beside the bed. She eased on to the floor and left the sleeping room, as Isaac called it.

Isaac was standing over the metal stove turning bacon with a knife.

"Good morning, Motesey," he said. "Striker and Weasel is up and has come in, but has gone back out to make water, I think. You drink coffee?"

248

He had a nice smile. "I name Me-ot-zi," she said. "No drink coffee. I go make water too."

"Sorry. Meotzi, right? Well, they's a little house out back aways you can use, if you like." He nodded toward the back door.

She remembered the little houses from her time at the fort with Custer. Soldiers called them 'shit houses.' They were disgusting, usually. Maybe his was better. His cabin was very clean. She went to the rear door, and backed out quietly.

It was barely dawn, and still dark outside. She closed the door and turned to look for the little house, but found herself staring at the painted face of a mounted Lakota warrior. She swallowed a scream. He loosed the tension on his bow string and signed for her to be quiet and move around front.

There she found Weasel and Striker surrounded by five more mounted Lakotas. Their leader looked like the one called Gall. The men were signing and whispering. She became aware of many more warriors in the growing light, some by the stream, some by the barn, others leading horses out of the corral.

"Hey," she said to the Lakota chief. "Those are our horses. Ours, and the white man who lives here. He's a friend. You can't rob us!"

"Hush, little one," said Weasel.

The Lakota chief said, "Shut up, woman!"

"No! I mean it. This man is giving White medicine to my son, who was shot in the Greasy Grass fight. You cannot have our horses and you must not hurt this man or steal from him. I will not let you."

"You won't? Somebody hit this woman in the mouth." The chief looked at Striker.

Striker said, "Please, Meotzi, just be quiet. This is Chief Gall. We are trying to tell . . ."

The front door of the cabin opened, and Isaac stepped out. "What's the commotion? What the hell? Meotzi?" He quickly made the peace sign, then wiped his hands on his apron.

"Meotzi? Did somebody say Meotzi?" Another Lakota detached himself from the horse thieves and rode over to the gathering in front of the store.

"White Bull. Now is a good time to see you," said Meotzi. "A very good time. Tell your friends who would take our horses who we are."

Cranky Bear Woman pushed her way past Isaac and shouted, "Don't kill us, Lakota men. Kill the White man if you want, but not us. We are *Tsi-Tsi-Tsas. Shahiyenas.* Friends. No kill, please."

Yellow Bird ducked by Isaac and Cranky Bear Woman and stepped in front of Meotzi. He held one hand to the bloody bandage on his head and the other behind him. "Who are these men, Mother? What do they want?"

"These are mighty Lakota warriors, my son. Fierce. Very brave. They want to steal our horses and rob our friend Isaac."

The boy pulled Meotzi's little pistol from behind him and pointed it at White Bull. Everyone heard him cock it. "I know you. You brought my mother gifts. Wanted us to live in your tipi. You would steal from us?"

"No, no, no," said White Bull. "Never. This is a mistake. Gall, these Shahiyenas were on the last hill with me, when I fought Yellow Hair. That one, Old Weasel, shot Yellow Hair in the head. With that pistol. And that boy is Yellow Hair's son."

More Lakotas had crowded in to hear the exchange, and what began as a murmur soon rose to a roar as the word spread.

"Enough!" shouted Gall. "I have heard of this woman and her boy, who was shot by Bluecoats. And her daughter, who was killed. This is Big Medicine. We take nothing from these people. Not ever. Little warrior, put your hammer down, but never lose that gun. May I hold it?"

Yellow Bird looked to Meotzi, who nodded. He marched over to Gall's horse and handed up the little Smith and Wesson.

Gall held it up for all to see and shouted, "The gun that killed Yellow Hair! Big Medicine!" He bent and handed it back to Yellow Bird and patted his head. "You have a strong heart, boy, like your mother. Get well. Grow. Take care of her. We go!" He wheeled away and led the yipping Lakotas through the stream and off toward the rising sun.

White Bull held back a moment as the others rode away. "Be careful, friends. Many Bluecoats are searching for us. They may follow us here. I think we'll circle around them and go up to where the Redcoats live. You could go with us. Meotzi, I would take care of you and the boy."

"My boy cannot travel yet. And you have a wife."

"And she's a good cook," White Bull said, grinning, "but she hurts my eyes, and you make my eyes happy. My bad luck." He rode away.

Meotzi hugged Yellow Bird, then faced Cranky Bear Woman. In Cheyenne she said, "Kill the White man? Really?"

The old woman whined, "It seemed like the smart thing to say. I wasn't really awake.

252

Weasel, help me here. She's picking on me again."

Meotzi shook her head in disgust. "Come on, Yellow Bird. We'll go to the woods and make water. You can protect me with that pistol. Then we'll change your head wrap and eat."

"Yes, Mother. Protect you from what?"

"Snakes. Wolves. Lakotas. Mean old women."

Striker

As Meotzi and Yellow Bird headed back to the woods, Isaac plopped down on a bench by his front door. He took a deep breath and blew it out. "Sweet Jesus," he started, then remembered to sign. "Many thanks, Cheyenne friends. I believe they would have killed me if you were not here."

Cranky Bear Woman snorted and scurried back inside, signing, "I go eat now."

Striker shook his head. "I can't believe she's my mother."

Weasel said, "I'm not sure I'm your father, but I know she's your mother."

"I can't believe you laid with her," said Striker. "And still do."

"Not so much anymore," Weasel said. "It is not something that I can talk to you about, but she is different under a buffalo

253

robe." He closed his eyes and smiled. "I remember once we were . . ."

Isaac interrupted. "I don't know much Sioux talk, even less Cheyenne. I could follow some of the signing. What were they saying about Yellow Hair? Is that Custer they's talking about?"

"Yes," Striker said. "There was a big fight. All the Lakota, many of us Tsi-Tsi-Tsas, many Bluecoats. Somebody," he glanced at Weasel, "killed Yellow Hair . . ."

"And somebody else killed his brother," signed Weasel. "Let us not forget that."

"Yes," Striker continued, "and many of his men."

"Lordamercy. Custer dead? How many soldiers killed?" Isaac stood and looked around, as if he expected vengeful Bluecoats to appear at any moment.

"Dead? Many, many. Like the trees in the forest. And now many more will come with their two-shooting guns to punish the Lakotas and Tsi-Tsi-Tsas. That is why we are leaving these Black Hills and going far that way." Striker pointed south. "Back to the Lodge Pole River."

"Two-shooting guns?"

"You Whites say cannons. Go bang two times," Weasel spoke with authority.

Striker stared at him. "You old pile of

buffalo droppings. You speak White talk?"

"Not so much. Mostly I listen. When you get old, you learn to do that."

Striker raised his hands in exasperation, then turned back to Isaac. "The warrior who shot Yellow Hair has much to fear from the Bluecoats. And he used that little pistol of Meotzi's. It's Big Medicine. If Whites learn of it, they may come and take it. Or maybe Crows will!"

"The man who killed Custer's brother better sleep with one eye open also," Weasel said. "You plan to tell this White man about Meotzi and Yellow Hair and the boy? How he is Yellow Hair's son? He may want us to leave if you do." Following Striker's lead, Weasel signed all that he spoke.

"We will find out very soon," Striker almost shouted, "Since you just told him. Do you forget Isaac can make signs?"

Isaac laughed at the exchange. "No. You must not leave yet. The boy should not travel for many more days. And if he is Custer's boy, he may be safe from both Whites and Indians."

CHAPTER TWENTY-NINE

Meotzi

"Look, Mother! Striker and Weasel are coming. They are riding fast. I think something is wrong."

Cranky Bear Woman and Isaac came out to join Meotzi and Yellow Bird as the two warriors splashed through the stream. Weasel held a fat young pronghorn in front of him and there was blood on his hands and legs.

As the men yanked their winded ponies to a halt, Cranky Bear Woman said, "Are you shot, old man?"

Weasel dropped the antelope at her feet and jumped down. "No. It's his blood. We had no time to bleed him out. Clean him, and put my horse away. I may need a fresh one."

"White men are coming," said Striker. "A wagon and five riders." He pointed toward the rising sun. "That way. You'll see them soon."

"Bluecoats?" Meotzi asked. "Do we hide?"

"No," said Weasel. "We used Striker's long-looking glass."

"Well, if they are not soldiers, why are you getting us so excited?" Meotzi stamped her foot. "There have been White men coming here almost every day, bringing furs and trading for supplies."

Striker grinned. "These are not all White men. One is black, and one is a woman . . ."

"And one is a White spirit man. Black Robe." Weasel interrupted, making the sign of the cross.

Striker continued, ". . . and the woman is not White. She is Serenity Killer, who was Black Kettle's slave. Remember?"

Meotzi nodded. "He gave her away. She became Shelly and married that black man at Balliett's Post. Bear? Wasn't that his name?"

"Yes. You are right. And I think this black man may be Bear, but he is heavier and looks older," Striker said.

"He is older, fool. It's been eight summers since we saw him. It was before I had Yellow Bird."

"Yes, Meotzi, you are right, but listen. I think the other two men might be Dobey and The Boss. From Balliett's Post," Striker said. "Lots of hair on their faces now, but I think it's them."

Meotzi turned to Isaac. "If he's right, these are good friends from long ago. From the Lodge Pole River area, where we are going."

Isaac said, "Well, I'm happy for you."

Meotzi noticed his eyes were not happy. Not at all.

CHAPTER THIRTY

Brick

"So, how come they call you Brick, if that ain't your real name?"

"Same ways they call you Blacky, when your real name is Black Dog Weathers. Blacky's just more easy to say. And to remember, I guess. It ain't got as many words and letters." The seven year old Bobby 'Brick' Walls shrugged as he said it, as if he really wasn't sure. He didn't want to seem like a durn know-it-all to his cousin Blacky.

Sometimes he felt smarter than Blacky who was more than a year older, but most times Blacky could make him feel like a durn moron. Since Blacky was grinning from ear to ear right now, Brick was pretty sure this was gonna be one of those times.

"Well, mister smarty-pants, that ain't why at all. My daddy says it's cause of your red hair. Says it looks like the red bricks they use in the walls of houses in big towns. See? Brick Walls. Kind of like your daddy's name, Dobey Walls, which is made up from Adobe and Walls."

Brick frowned. "Well, I ain't ever seen no red bricks, so how's I to know? I bet you ain't seen one neither . . ."

The two boys were fishing for catfish on the south bank of the Canadian River, less than a mile from their home. Best friends, they argued constantly and were generally corrected by their other best friend, eleven year old Tommy Christmas.

Tommy was Brick's half-brother. He would have been with them today, but he was on sentry duty with eight year old Millie, who was half-sister to both Brick and Tommy. Their other best friend Billy Ridges was sick.

The argument was interrupted by Brick's cane pole being snatched from his hands. Blacky dropped his own pole and grabbed Brick's before it could be pulled away.

"Big 'un!" he yelled, as he planted his heels and started to pull. Sliding down the bank, he yelled again. "Quick! Grab my 'spenders!"

Brick scrambled to his feet, hooked his right forearm through Blacky's suspenders and wrapped his other arm around a young cottonwood tree. Between them, they hauled in their best catch ever.

"Lookit that," said Blacky. "That's a ten-pounder, I betcha."

"It's my fish," said Brick.

"It's our fish," said somebody, behind them. As Brick turned, he thought, whoever it is, he kind of talks like Aunt Manuela. And Aunt Carmela. When he faced the man, Brick almost tumbled backwards into the river.

The man wore a black hat with silver conchos and despite the summer heat, a black vest over a white shirt. There was a bone-handled revolver on one hip and a large bone-handled knife on the other. He also wore an evil smile, made more fearsome by some missing teeth. A leather quirt was lashed to his left wrist and he slapped his leg with it as he grinned at the boys.

"Hey," said Blacky, "I knows you. You used to work here. Horsebreaker, with my Daddy. You're Mickey, ain't you? I mean, Mister Ortega?"

"Yeah," said Brick. "I 'member you too. Durn, mister, you 'bout scared the mess out of us."

The man nodded and continued to grin as he fingered what looked like six mushrooms on the thong around his neck. He took the squirming catfish from Blacky, placed it on the ground and held it down with his boot, then drew that big knife and stabbed it through the gills. It quit squirming.

He finally spoke. "*Si*. I am Ortega. *Senor* Ortega to you. And yes, I did work here, until somebody snuck up on me and knocked my teeth out. And fired me, when I didn't do nothing wrong. All because somebody's wife was drunk and wanted to play, and he thought I started it."

Brick couldn't figure out what he was talking about. He started to say that sure didn't seem fair, but just then a second man stepped out of the bushes. He was older, a scruffy white man with bad teeth and a droopy mustache.

"Ain't nobody coming, Mickey," he said. He pulled off his straw hat and wiped his forehead with his sleeve.

Brick noticed his brown hair was dirty as was his neck and shirt. It occurred to him, maybe for the first time, that the men he knew closely, his daddy, Uncle Boss, Uncle Bear, Cherokee Jim, Doc, and Uncle Tad, all washed up 'bout every day. Heck, so did the old black men, George Canada and Big William. Of course the women did, and all them grownups made sure all the young 'uns cleaned up too. Said that's why hardly nobody got sick. 'Cept Billy, and that was 'cause probably he drank water downstream from where some horse or cow had shit, or so his daddy thought. Give Billy the drizzling shits himself . . .

Ortega's quirt upside his head brought Brick back to the river bank. "What you dreaming, boy? You wake up. I'm talking to you."

Brick said, "Yessir. I'm sorry. I was thinking . . ."

"Don't think, *Pinejo*. Listen. You like my little ear collection?" He fingered one of those things he wore around his neck.

"Ears?" said Blacky. "I thought they was mushrooms or something."

Brick stared. He couldn't speak.

"No mushrooms, *Muchacho*. These are Apache ears. Six ears. One *senora,* one *muchacho,* one *muchacha.* Their scalps I sold to the *Federales,* but I keep the ears. And I think I would like maybe some little *Gringo* ears. Maybe some *Negrito* ears too." He licked his lips and stared hard at Blacky, who backed away, slipped in the mud, and slid into the edge of the slow moving river.

"Grab aholt of him, Dave. Bring him here," Ortega ordered. "Boys, meet Dirty Dave. He's one of my gang, and he don't care for rich boys no more'n I do."

Dirty Dave shoved the muddy, soppy Blacky up to Ortega, who grabbed an ear and twisted it.

"Yeah. This would look good on my string, wouldn't it? Maybe you two don't have no money, but you, boy," he nodded at Brick, "your mama and papa, they got some. They got lots of it. And you're gonna go get it for me, and bring it here. Ain't you?"

Blacky said, "Ouch. You's hurting me."

Brick said, "I know where it is, but if I take it, I'll get beat."

Ortega shook the quirt in his face. "If you don't, I will cut this one's ears off. And his balls. And then we'll come in there and do the same to you. And we'll have some fun with your mamas, before we cut them up and kill 'em. See, we know your papas and most of your fighters is gone. I got two men watching your fort right now." He nodded and smiled that terrible snaggle-tooth grin and let that sink in. "We could just ride in there, kill ever 'body and take whatever's there, but all I really wants is the *dinero,* see? Nobody gets hurt. You bring it, we takes you off a little ways and lets you walk home. And you don't never tell what happened or we come back and catch you just like we did today. Only then we'll cut up

264

ever'body and kill 'em. *Comprende?* You un-nerstand me?"

Both boys nodded, wide-eyed with fear.

"I'll just keep little Black Dog here. You go, get it and get back here before dark, so's no one is looking for him. Get all of it, *Muchacho.* You don't want me to come back. We're just gonna set here and fry us up some catfish. Now, git. *Andele!*"

Black Dog

Brick was supposed to be back long before dark, but it still seemed like two days to Blacky. A third bandit showed up to eat after Brick left to go steal the money. The others called him Brushy Bill, and Blacky didn't like the way he looked. Or acted.

The slick-haired man kept smiling at him, and making kissing lips, like Aunt Honey would do. And winking too, like her. Blacky had never seen a man act like that, so he'd just look away. Then the man pointed at him and whispered something to Ortega. Dirty Dave frowned and Ortega stared at Blacky for a few seconds, then shook his head.

Brushy Bill said, "Well, shit, Mickey. Why not? He might like it, and 'sides, who's gonna tell? Not him, for damn sure. You gonna tell? How 'bout you, Dirty Dave, you want it spread around that you poked a

265

nigger-Indian boy?"

Dirty Dave just shrugged and said, "I don't do that, and it don't matter none 'cause there ain't no time. Here comes Gore with the other boy."

Brick pulled off his hat which was packed full of paper bills. Gore pushed him away and started counting it.

Ortega pointed his quirt at Brick and said, "You saying that's all?"

"Nossir," said Brick. "I ain't said nothing. There's more." He unshucked his shirt, and more bills fell on the ground. A lot of them. Then be began pulling more from his pockets.

When he stopped, Dirty Dave whistled, then shoved him toward Blacky and said, "Go set with your little nigger friend."

Brick took the same position as Blacky, cross-legged on the ground, then whispered, "You all right, Blacky?"

Blacky said, "Why'd you take so long? I think they mean to poke out our eyes, Brick. I'm plumb scared."

"Our eyes? I thought they just wanted to cut off our ears . . ."

"Just cut off our ears? Damn, white boy, do you hear what you're saying?"

"Y'all shut the hell up over there!" Ortega yelled at them. "No more whispering. And where's the gold? Them buffalo runners always paid in coin."

"Yessir, I was . . ." Brick stuttered as he stood. "But he told me to come set down, and . . ." Brick unhooked his belt and slid off a sock he had tied to it and hung inside his paints. "There it is. He didn't let me finish . . ." He tossed the sock to Ortega, who sliced it open and dumped the coins on the hard earth.

Brick tucked in his shirt, re-hooked his belt and dropped beside Blacky again. "I was hoping they wouldn't think of no coins," he whispered.

"Nice try," whispered Blacky. "Maybe now they won't poke us in the eyes."

"Godalmighty, Ortega, there's over a thousand dollars here." Gore stood and punched Brushy Bill in the shoulder. "Hot damn, Bill, think on that. Even split four ways, that's way over a hundred fifty each."

"Yeah," said Brushy Bill. "And we still got these boys to play with . . ."

"We ain't playing with no boys," Dirty Dave cut in. "I don't wanna hear no more talk about it. We needs to let these boys go afore someone comes a-looking for 'em, and git the hell out of here."

"What's go you so high and mighty? How 'about you tell me the difference between bending these boys over, or bending over some whore in Sweetwater?" Brushy Bill started to get up from where he knelt.

Dirty Dave pushed him down with his left hand. With his right, he drew and cocked a long-barreled Richards Colt and held it beside his leg. He said, "Now, I don't know whether you come to such behavior in a orphanage or in prison, but it don't please me. Not none at all. You push, and we'll be splitting this three ways, 'stead of four. These boys done what we ast, so now we let 'em go and we ride. Ain't that right, Ortega?"

Ortega waved his quirt at the boys. "Yeah, we do that, but you *muchachos* see how it is with my gang. You tell anybody what happened, I'll come back and let Brushy Bill have you before I take your ears."

Both boys nodded. Hard, and a lot, but Brushy Bill said, "You ain't gonna just leave 'em here, is you? If you ain't gonna kill 'em, we oughta at least carry 'em off a few miles so's they has to walk back and give us some kind of a lead."

Dirty Dave added, "Yeah, Ortega, that's what you said to begin with, anyways. And on top of that, ain't nobody got a long gun 'cept me. And all I got is that Kentucky rifle, if they come after us."

"Yeah," snorted Gore. "A durn muzzle loader. Forty-two caliber, at that. Ain't even a good deer gun."

Dirty Dave said, "Yeah? And what did you bring to the dance? Let's go. Let 'em ride with me and Gore. Else you'll have Brushy Bill trying out fornication in the saddle."

The bandits dropped them five miles south of Canadian Fort, about an hour before dark. As the boys started that long walk home, Blacky said, "I don't think they was talking about poking us in the eye."

Brick gave him his grown-up know-it-all shrug, but said, "Who knows, cousin? And what's fornification?"

"Heck, Brick, I don't know. I ain't no bandit. Don't look back, now. Might make 'em change they minds and come after us."

"I got to pee, Blacky."

"Not now, Brick. Not whilst they can see us."

"I got to pee real bad. And how we gonna know when they can't see us, if we can't look back?"

"They come after us, you'll piss in your pants. Just walk. They's some bushes up ahead. Leastways, hold it till then, and I'll take a look." Blacky led out at a fast pace.

"Durn," said Brick, struggling to keep up,

"I ain't likely to ever go fishing again."

They never made it home by full dark, but the grown-ups were out looking for them. They heard Cherokee Jim yelling their names four miles out, answered him, and he soon had them up on his horse, Brick in front and Blacky on the horse's rump.

As he turned his Appaloosa toward home, Cherokee Jim drew a revolver and banged off two rounds toward they sky. Both boys jumped.

"Two shots means I got both of you and you're all right. One shot woulda meant only one found, and three or more woulda meant to come to me, 'cause somebody's hurt. Now, why on earth was you down here? Wasn't you supposed to be fishing, other side of town?"

"Yessir, but we got to chasing a jack rabbit and got lost in the dark. We is both really sorry. Ain't we, Brick?"

"Yessir. Really sorry. And hungry. Is mama mad?"

Brick

After they were fed and fussed at and fussed over, Brick finally crept into the bed he shared with Tommy Christmas.

Tommy said, "You didn't make a lot of

270

sense in there, little brother. You gonna tell me what truly happened?"

"I can't, Tommy. I can't never talk about it. I did something bad, but I had to 'cause of Blacky. And I can't tell you no more. Not never."

"Did Blacky make you do it, whatever it is?"

"Naw, Tommy, he didn't make me do nothing, but what I did was because of him. I can't explain it no better than that. And Tommy, I'm real tired."

CHAPTER THIRTY-ONE

Brick

Somebody with bad teeth was trying to poke Brick in the eyes with a stick, and he was having trouble moving his head to dodge the jabs. He twisted and groaned.

Blacky shook him some more, saying, "Brick! Brick! You got to wake up! They's back!"

Brick rubbed his eyes and said, "Who's back? Back where?" He sat up and looked around.

"Ortega and them. He's in the store, and they's out front, that's who. Get up. Come on."

Brick shushed him and said, "Where's Tommy?"

Blacky said, "He was on watch with me. When I seen them bandits ride up I left him to come get you."

"What're we gonna do, Blacky?"

"Let's slip in the kitchen and see can we

hear what Ortega's saying. Come on, get dressed."

"Hey, wait a minute. I was s'posed to be on watch, not Tommy." Brick scrambled into his clothes.

"I know you was, but we couldn't wake you up, so Tommy took your place."

In the kitchen, Brick huddled in fear with Blacky, as they watched Ortega shopping for a rifle from his mama. Behind them, Cherokee Jim sipped his morning coffee with Big William.

Cherokee Jim

"You still gonna hunt me up some meat this morning?" Big William stood as he finished his coffee.

Cherokee Jim pushed away from the table and stood too. "That's my plan. You spare some jerky, in case my hunt runs long?"

Big William grinned. "Got you a pouch already made up. Why don't you take them two nosey boys there, and get 'em outa my kitchen."

The boys faced Cherokee Jim as if they hadn't noticed anyone else in the room, even though they'd rushed between him and the cook when they came in the back door minutes earlier. The look on their faces put him on alert. He pushed through the curtain into the store.

Mickey Ortega stood at the counter, leering at Honey, who said, "I don't know what you're talking about. Do you want to buy something or not?"

Cherokee Jim noticed that Honey was blushing and seemed mad. It didn't sit well with him. While he'd never had a face-off with Ortega, the man had disappeared suddenly some time back and left the place shorthanded. He also suspected Ortega had been forward with Mandy, though she wouldn't confirm it. Maybe the man had made a pass at Honey too and been run off. Whatever, Cherokee Jim didn't care much for him.

As he entered the room, he picked up his Yellowboy carbine from behind the counter and made a small show of levering a round into the chamber and lowering the hammer, looking straight at Ortega as he did.

"Ortega. Long time. You ain't showing as many teeth as you did last time I seen you. You here on business, or just bothering the women?"

Ortega flashed his smile. "I'm here to buy me a rifle. One of them new '73 models. Not some old Indian gun like you carry."

Cherokee Jim passed behind him to stand

near the door as Honey took an 1873 Winchester rifle from the rack and handed it to Ortega. Ortega worked the action a few times, ordered a box of .44-40 cartridges for it and a box of .45 Colt for his revolver. He paid up and swaggered out, giving Cherokee Jim an insolent smile. When he tried to tip his hat to Honey, he dropped the two boxes of ammunition. They popped open and scattered cartridges on the floor.

Honey laughed. Cherokee Jim said, "I like my old Yellowboy because it uses the same bullets as my pistol. I don't have to buy two boxes, and then drop them and look stupid and all."

Ortega's face was livid with hate and embarrassment as he knelt and scrambled to pick up his spill and jam the cartridges back into their boxes. He rushed out to his horse and struggled to stuff the boxes in a saddlebag while holding his new rifle under one arm.

Cherokee Jim followed him out, smiling at his discomfort. "You sure you don't want to come back in and ask Miz Honey for a scabbard to put your new rifle in? I'm sure she'd sell you one."

Ortega glared at him. "I can carry it, I reckon. And you can go straight to hell, you damn Cherokee." He wheeled away and kicked his horse into a lope through the gate. The other three men followed him.

Honey

As soon as she lifted the hearth stone, she knew something was wrong. Most of the paper money was gone and a box of coins was near empty. She rushed to check the other two stashes and found them intact, but at least a thousand was missing from the first site.

Within fifteen minutes Honey had checked with all of the adults in the 'family.' Tad said maybe Dobey and Boss Melton had taken it for their trip up to Dakota Territory, but Honey and her mother had counted out their traveling money and besides, the missing money had been there as late as yesterday.

She grabbed Tommy Christmas and said, "I want you to ride over to Hog Town and ask Doc to come here. Tell him it's real important."

The boy said, "What's the matter, Mama Honey? All the grown-ups is acting upset."

She said, "I guess you might as well know. A bunch of money is gone from one of our hiding places. I got to see did Doc borry it or something."

"Money's gone? Somebody took it? You think it was them men was here this morning?"

"No, I don't," she said. "None of them was anywhere near the stash. Though that Ortega did flash some money. But if it was ours, he had to get it from somebody who knew where it was hid."

She saw the boy had become very nervous. "You don't think one of us give it to them, do you, Mama Honey?"

"I don't know what to think right now. Do you know something about this? You're acting mighty strange."

"No, no, not really. I mean, really I don't know nothing. But what if somebody made somebody do it 'cause they was scared? Could that be it, maybe?"

She stared hard at him. "Are you saying you gave our money to those men because they scared you?"

"No. No, ma'am. I mean, maybe somebody did. But not me. Why do you think it was me?"

" 'Cause you brought it up, young man. And it maybe is the only explanation. Do what I said, take your pony and go get Doc over here. Go bareback. Don't fool with no saddle. And I ain't through with you."

Honey ran outside and caught Cherokee

Jim, saddled and ready for his hunt.

"Any luck, Miz Honey? Is it really missing?"

"Jim, I think those men, Ortega and his little gang, I think they paid me with our own money. I think they did something to scare Tommy Christmas into giving it up to 'em."

"You ain't serious. Are you?" He mounted and said, "I'll go after 'em."

"I think you have to," Honey said, "but I sent Tommy to fetch Doc. I need to ask him first did he take it, but I got a bad feeling. Why don't you wait and get a horse ready for Doc so's you and him can take out after them soon as he gets here? In case he didn't borry it."

Cherokee Jim

Doc said, "I just don't see how we'll catch up to them moving as slowly as we are. I mean, I know I'm no help as far as reading their tracks, but we know they rode toward Sweetwater. And they have at least a two hour head start."

Cherokee Jim said, "It's not easy to pick up their tracks, mixed all in with ours from last night. Now, their tracks will pull away from ours when we get to where we found the boys, maybe four miles out. But I have

278

to watch for them pulling away, either east or west, before we reach that point."

"So, we're looking for hoof prints heading off to the right or left?"

"Yeah, Doc, prob'ly four sets of prints, as they didn't have no packhorse. Unless they split up."

"You mean, you can't distinguish between their tracks and ours? What kind of frontiersman are you? And you're an Indian." Doc shock his head, clearly disgusted.

Cherokee Jim smiled. "I just ain't that good. See, if one of 'em has lost a shoe, or maybe one has hooves that's lots bigger or smaller than the others, I can spot that, but so far they look about the same." He pulled up, moved off to the right several yards and dismounted.

"So," Doc said, "have you discovered a variance of some recognizable sort?"

"What I've discovered is a string of horse turds heading west. Looks like three or four ponies maybe going towards Adobe Walls, 'stead of Sweetwater." Cherokee Jim remounted and kicked his pony into a lope. "Got to be them."

As Doc caught up, he said, "This is more like it. How did these scoundrels get to the money, anyhow? It's not like the women to let anyone into the living areas."

"I don't think they did this time, neither. Miz Honey tole me she thinks that Ortega scared Tommy Christmas into giving it to 'em."

"I find that hard to believe," said Doc. "That boy seems to have more character than that. Now tell me what you plan to do if we do catch up to these men."

Cherokee Jim said, "I mean to search them and find that money. Either before or after we kill them."

Late that afternoon Doc said, "Perhaps we'll spot them once we top that bluff up ahead."

Cherokee Jim said, "Maybe. More likely we'll spot their fire when they make camp in a couple of hours. If they make camp. If they ain't already spotted us. Matter of fact, Doc, that mesa would be a good place for an ambush . . ."

The bullet hit Cherokee Jim's horse in the chest and dropped him before he heard the crack of the rifle, but he saw the bloom of white smoke as he sailed over the Appaloosa's neck. The shooter was on the mesa, maybe eighty yards away.

He threw his hands out to break the fall and jammed his right thumb enough to make him yell.

Doc was carrying the long Remington

.50-70 that Jim had planned to hunt with. He banged off a round toward the smoke on the bluff, then dismounted and snatched a cartridge pouch from his saddle horn. He slapped his bay's rump then took cover behind Jim's down pony just as Jim did.

"Give 'em another shot so's I can snatch my carbine," Cherokee Jim said.

Doc fired again, then said, "Your mount is slobbering blood and froth. I fear he's lung shot."

"I think so too, Doc, but what I fear is he'll roll over on us." Jim rose to his knees and shot his pony in the head. The horse trembled, went stiff legged, then was still.

"There's been no return fire," said Doc. "Perhaps I hit someone. I heard you cry out. You're not hit, are you?"

"I'm not, but I hurt my thumb so bad I near screamed like a girl. It don't seem broke, but I ain't got much use of it."

Doc took his hand and twisted and turned the thumb.

"Yeoww!" Cherokee Jim whispered.

"It's not broken but you'll probably have to use your left thumb to cock your pistol for a while. Or perhaps just shoot left-handed."

The rifle on the bluff cracked again, and dirt flew up near Doc's horse which was now grazing about thirty yards away.

"The scoundrels are trying to knock down my horse too!" Doc shouted. He rose up to fire, but Cherokee Jim was already kneeling and sending a blistering stream of .44's toward the white smoke on the mesa. As he levered and fired he also delivered a blistering stream of Cherokee profanity.

Doc got off two more shots from the Rolling Block before Jim said, "Hold fire. They's running. Gimme that long gun."

He took the gun, cocked it, rolled back the breech, and pushed in another fat cartridge. He closed the breech, then flipped up the ladder sight and set it on two hundred yards. He said, "Stand up, Doc, lemme rest this over your shoulder. And watch your ears."

The Remington bucked and roared, and the smoke completely blocked their view.

"Did you get one? Did you get one?"

"Hell, Doc, I can't see no more'n you can. Hang on, now, looks like only three horses running. Doc, you stay here, cover me with this." He thrust the long gun back into Doc's hands. "I'm gonna grab your horse and ride up there, see if maybe I dropped one."

As he ran to Doc's horse, Jim yelled over his shoulder, "Go ahead and shoot some, pin 'em down. I'll ride to them rocks on the right of 'em."

In minutes, Cherokee Jim was dismounted at the rock outcrop on the mesa. He could see why the men had chosen their ambush position instead of the rocks he was in. At least two rattlers were buzzing away at him, and there could have been more snakes. The ambush had been set up in a depression, probably an old buffalo wallow, thirty yards away.

The three riders were disappearing into the gloom, best part of a mile away. But just thirty yards beyond the wallow, a blue roan was down and Jim could see a man's leg kicking at the saddle. Pinned under?

He tried to reload his Yellowboy, but that durn thumb gave him a fit. He figured he still had five rounds in the carbine and there were five more in the Colt on his hip. He stood and waved his hat at Doc to stop his covering fire. Too late.

Several things happened in that next instant. Doc fired again, the ambusher kicked free and stood, waving a pistol, and Jim shot him. Dust flew off his leg and his stomach and he went down.

Jim waved at Doc again and got a return wave, then approached the bandit.

"Don't make me shoot you again, mister."

The man groaned and said, "It's too late. I'm shot to pieces. Can I get some water?"

Jim took the man's revolver and knife, then looked him over. One leg was twisted and bleeding, and he was hit in one arm and in the belly. Through and through.

"Water will kill you since you're gut shot. But I guess it don't matter. Being gutshot, you're gonna die anyways." Jim pulled a canteen off the man's horse and handed it to him. "Was you with Ortega?'

The dying man guzzled water and nodded. "I was, right up 'til he left me. I hope you catch him and kill him. Durn half-breed bastard."

"You didn't make that no easier for me, shooting my horse. I'll have to ride home with my partner and get fresh mounts, then start over again."

"Well, I wasn't aiming at your horse. I's trying to hit you. All I had was my old muzzle loader, and besides, you kilt my horse. And me. I'd say we's more'n even. Hell, one of you 'bout shot my leg clean off."

Cherokee Jim smiled. "I might of liked you, if you hadn't of taken a bandit's path. How come Ortega wasn't raining hell on us with that new Winchester?"

The man coughed and spat. "You ain't

gonna even believe this. The fool didn't go to load the durn thing 'til y'all come in sight, and then he jams a .45 Colt cartridge in the loading gate. Won't go in, won't come out, so what's he do next? Broke the tip off his knife blade, trying to unscrew the side plate so's he could clear it." He drank some more water and said, "Lord, my belly hurts. How much time I got? Y'all gonna finish me or just leave me?"

Doc walked up then, breathing heavy from climbing the mesa. He heard the last question, and raised his eyebrows at Cherokee Jim. "Our outlaw friend doesn't look too well, does he?"

"Done told him he's dying, Doc, but I dunno how long he's got."

The man tried to sit up. "You're a doc? Can you help me?"

Doc sniffed the man's stomach, then rolled him on his side to look at the exit wound. "It's as I thought," he said. "There's feces in the blood under you. You have perhaps a day, no more."

"Well, ain't that the way of it. Lookit, y'all get my traps, saddle, and guns and all. Only fair you don't let the coyotes finish me. And shoot me in the back of the head, so's I don't see it coming."

Cherokee Jim said, "I'll do that for you.

What's your name, and who do you want told?"

"I won't say. Don't want nobody to know how I went. Used to be a purty good soldier, 'til I took a wrong turn, like you said. Listen, now, y'all don't be too hard on them two little boys who give us the money. Ortega told 'em he'd cut off their peckers and cut up their mommas if they held out."

Doc said, "You've just earned your quick departure from this sad life. Thank you for telling us."

"Yessir, but I got one question before I go. What are feces?"

Doc told him.

"Oh, Hell," the dying man said, shuddering. "I'm done here. Go on and finish me."

CHAPTER THIRTY-TWO

Honey

Annette set a plate in front of Brick, then used a knife to spear him a large hot biscuit. She ladeled some red-eye gravy on it as he broke it open, and Honey added two slices of fried ham.

"Now eat all your breakfast while me and your grandma have some coffee and talk. Wash your plate when you're through." Honey ruffled his hair, then joined Annette at the other table.

Annette started. "So you think it was Tommy Christmas?"

"I don't know what else to make of it, Mama Balliett," Honey said. "He swears he didn't do it, but he's surely hiding something. That's as clear as the nose on his face. I don't know why he don't just own up. It ain't like he took it for himself, or got no benefit from it."

Annette shook her head. "Probably just

ashamed 'cause they scared him so bad."

Honey said, "Well, I chewed his little butt raw but got nowhere with him. Sent him to guard duty with no supper, and tole him just wait and see what his daddy would do when he comes home. And I said he'd better pray that didn't nothing bad happen to Cherokee Jim or Doc, out chasing them scoundrels."

Honey realized Brick had left his food untouched and was standing in front of her.

"Mama, is it a lie when you know something and don't say it?"

"No, son, but it's like a lie. Might as well be one."

"Do you go to Hell for it?" He was fidgeting like he had to pee.

"No. Listen to me. You ain't going to Hell. Now what is it you know and ain't said? Did you see Tommy Christmas take that money?"

"Tommy didn't take that money, Mama."

"Well, who did it then?" She almost shouted. "It didn't walk outta here on its own two feet, now did it?"

Brick burst into tears. "I did it, Mama. But them men had Blacky. They said they'd cut off his pizzle and ears if I didn't, and hurt you and Aunt Shelly and everybody. I didn't give 'em all of it, like they said to.

288

Just some. We was so scared. And Tommy took the blame and we didn't say nothing. Don't hate him, Mama. Tommy didn't do nothing wrong. Didn't lie or nothing, just let you think he done it."

Shelly came in, looking worried. "Black Dog has run away."

Honey said, "I think I know why. Brick, do you know where he might go?" She turned to face her son, but he was gone.

Black Dog

Black Dog could see things had changed in the half-day since he ran away. A lot. His mother and Aunt Honey had stern faces and Tommy looked sort of happy. First time Tommy had seemed all right since them men came. Black Dog sat down on a bench beside Brick in Aunt Honey's living room.

"Sorry 'bout the mud," he said. "Brick caught me a ways downstream. I can't seem to do nothing right. Brick says y'all know everything, and we ain't going to Hell."

"Giving up the money wasn't so wrong," his mother said. "Letting us blame Tommy was the bad thing. But Tommy says he don't hold it against you two. And you're home safe, so I think we're all right."

"Yes," said Aunt Honey, squeezing Tommy's arm. "We are. We surely are."

"Well," said Black Dog, looking around. "I see y'all still got that same old cat. What's for supper?"

CHAPTER THIRTY-THREE

Cherokee Jim

"So that's how it happened," Cherokee Jim said, looking at Doc for confirmation. "I put him out of his misery, and we both got on Doc's horse, and then we figured out we would do better to come here than to go home. You being so close to their track and all. So here we is."

The two men were sitting in the large living room of the main house of Ostrich Ranch. Across from them were Willi Baranov, the owner, and his partner/manager Major Lang. A day and a half had passed since Jim's horse has been shot out from under him.

"Yes," Doc added, "and we need two fresh mounts, and perhaps a spare, so this doesn't happen again. I'll be happy to pay for them."

Willi waved the thought away. "You will not pay. But we have some problems too, yes? Maybe from these same men . . ."

The big major broke in. "Ja, I think so. A worker has rode here to tell us one cattle has been killed for food and twenty more taken. He says they were driven south, toward Sweetwater. I am just ready to ride after them when you are seen coming here, and we are thinking maybe you are the thieves coming back for more mischief. So I am waiting, but now I am thinking we will go to Sweetwater all together and catch these thiefs."

"All together?" Said Cherokee Jim.

"You, me, him," Lang said, jerking a thumb at Doc. "Willi, he will stay here with our workers. Watch for they come back."

An hour later, the three men rode south. Cherokee Jim pulled the pack horse. Major Lang sent two ranch hands north to retrieve saddles and tack from the dead horses of Jim and the bandit, and to bury the bandit.

As they rode, Cherokee Jim made note of their arms. He had his Yellowboy and Colt. Doc still had Jim's long Remington, with a ten gauge sawed-off double in his scabbard and a cut-down Navy conversion on his hip. Doc still liked those small grips on the Navy Colts. The Major had two Smith and Wessons in pommel holsters, and a shortened Schofield model in an under-arm holster. His main gun was a brand new '76 Winchester rifle in .45-75 caliber. A real hammer, Jim thought, and a good weapon for a big man.

Fifteen miles north of Sweetwater they met a cavalry patrol led by a grizzled Negro sergeant, his white hair and mustache a stark contrast to his bronze face.

"I see you done got the word, Doc," he said.

"What word is that, Whitey?"

"That young lawman over to Sweetwater, he come out to the fort, and asked the Cap'n could he send a message with the next patrol heading to Fort Dodge. Said to tell you folks at Balliett's Post that he might need some help. Some breed name of Ortega got a small gang and been raising sand down here. You didn't hear that?"

"I did not, but that would be the very gang of rascals we are trailing. Thank you, and when you get to Balliett's Post, please advise them what we're up to."

"Yassuh, Doc. Cherokee, y'all be careful, you hear? See you on the way back maybe."

They found Sheriff Buck Watson in his small office in front of his four-cell jail. He was sharing a bowl of stew with Junebug.

"She has to bring my food here for now, seeing as I got one of Ortega's men in back,

293

sobering up." Buck smiled suddenly and said, "I'm durn glad y'all are here. Doc, go in back there, see do you recognize my prisoner. The others wouldn't know him."

Junebug poured coffee all around, and Doc was back in no time. He took a mug too, stared hard at Junebug, and got barely a glance back. Cherokee Jim exhaled and breathed some easier.

Doc said, "Now I remember. He is that spineless lawman in Jacksboro. The one we ran off, what, six or seven years ago?"

Buck slapped the table. " 'Zactly right, Doc. Now he's running with Ortega. Getting kind of bold, what with Ortega flashing money, threatening me behind my back, and talking about putting this man in as the new law."

"What's this one named? I don't remember it from that Jacksboro incident." Doc jerked a thumb toward the cell behind him.

"Gore," said Buck. "Ike Gore. Him and his brother Billy and Brushy Bill Holder is who runs with Ortega. Had another one, Dirty Dave Clayborn, but I think that's who you killed in the ambush. They was all gone for a week or so, but the others come back a couple days ago, and ain't nobody seen Dirty Dave."

"Way you described the dead one, he had

to be Dirty Dave," Junebug said. "Ain't none of the others got an ounce of sand. And this one we got here, Ike, he couldn't of been with them others up around your place. He was in the jug here when they left and is back in now."

"Yeah," said Buck. "He was loaded again and bragging how he was gonna be the new law and waving a pistol and all. I whacked him and locked up him and his guns."

Cherokee Jim said, "And where do we find his partners?"

"Cantina over by Oscar Clanton's Stable and Corral, when they ain't out stealing," Buck replied. "I could just cut Ike loose and we follow him to 'em. He ain't gonna be no help to nobody, hung over and unarmed as he is."

Doc said, "Have you no deputies?"

"One," Buck said. "He's old, tired and asleep. He was on all night whilst I slept. They's a 'special policeman' the new mayor appointed, but don't neither one of 'em, him or the mayor, care for me none. They looks out for the gambling crowd and the likes of Ortega. Policeman's name is Beman."

Junebug said, "Best leave him out of it, Buck. Cut Ike loose and pay that Cogburn boy a dime to tail him and tell us where they is."

Buck

"You gimme my durn guns, Watson. You got no right to keep 'em, and you knows it." Ike Gore was still half drunk and blustery.

"Don't matter what's right, you ain't getting them, Ike. Come back full sober and pay my fine and then we'll talk," Buck said. "Right now you can just go cry to your friends. Me not giving you your guns is liable to keep you from getting shot."

"Wait 'til I'm the durn sheriff. We'll run you and your little lady friend outta here on a rail." Ike turned and shoved Cherokee Jim aside and headed for the door. "Damn Injin, stay outta my way."

Cherokee Jim said, "Touch me again, you better be heeled. For that matter, you speak to me again, you better have something in your hand."

Ike wheeled around and said, "That's bold talk from a small-fry redskin."

Cherokee Jim smashed the butt of his carbine into Ike's face, and said, "What did I say?"

Ike stumbled back two steps and went down flat on his back, his nose pouring blood. He groaned and grabbed the doorsill to pull himself erect.

Buck said, "Now you got blood on my floor and assaulted one of my new deputies. That's gonna be another twenty-five added to your fine. You want to try for fifty?"

Ike held his kerchief to his nose and mumbled, "That little push? You call that assault?"

Buck grinned, "Naw. I'm talking about you hitting him in the buttstock with your face. Now git!"

Doc

Little Bert Cogburn was back in twenty minutes. "He went by the barber, got him a plaster on his nose, then went straight to Pablo's Cantina, over by the O.C. Corral. And when I's coming back here I run into Officer Beman. He wanted to know if I'd seen Ortega's gang and was they armed."

Buck said, "Well?"

"I tole him they was in that open lot by the cantina and they all was carrying. Ike Gore won't wearing a gunbelt, but he checked his Winchester and put it in his saddle scabbard while I watched."

Buck said, "Y'all is deputized. Say 'I do' and we'll walk down there."

A block from the cantina, Beman rushed up to Buck and said, "No need to go down there, Watson. I've disarmed them, and they're saddled up and leaving town."

Buck brushed him aside and said, "We'll see. They want to pass on trouble and just ride out, we'll let 'em ride. And we'll follow 'em to wherever they hid them stolen coins. And cows."

Beman said, "I'm telling you, Buck, ain't no cause for a fight and I'll tell the mayor I warned you."

Buck said, "And I'm telling you, Beman, you line up with them cowboys and somebody shows a gun, I'll shoot you first."

Beman moved to the wooden walkway and dropped back as the four lawmen approached the empty side lot.

Buck said, "Doc, why don't you ease out to the right so's they don't ride out, sudden like, and surround us." It wasn't a request.

Doc thought, *Funny taking orders from a boy that used to be scared of me.* As he moved across the street, Doc was able to see deeper into the lot before the other lawmen could. His own tension had eased by half on hearing the cowboys were disarmed and mounted to leave. Buck, Cherokee Jim, and the Major had each been carrying a revolver in their right hands until they met Beman, but had re-holstered them.

In the empty lot between Oscar Clanton's

office and the cantina, Doc saw a saddled horse, then another, then four men standing in the middle of the lot, backs to him. One turned. Ike. The others spun too. Two gunbelts, and Ike easing toward a horse with a Winchester in a scabbard. The fourth man wore a long vest which could have covered a pistol.

"Buck," Doc said, "Four of them. They're not mounted. They are armed." He cocked both barrels of the ten gauge.

Now the other lawmen could see into the side lot too. Buck, over his shoulder, said, "Beman, you lying piece of buffalo shit . . ." Then to the four cowboys, "Y'all freeze. We're here to disarm you. Maybe talk about some stolen cattle and money."

Buck and Cherokee Jim both drew and cocked their revolvers, with Cherokee Jim using that two-handed hold so he could cock with his left thumb.

"Billy Gore, you're a boy. Ain't no need for you to die here, and you not eighteen yet. Step out. Won't nobody here back-shoot you," Buck said.

Major Lang finally pulled his pistol too.

The cowboys began to spread out. Ortega and a youngster each drew a revolver and held them down against their legs. Ike Gore's mare must have sensed he was nervous as she began to fidget and twist. Doc could see Ike was trying to reach a Winchester in the saddle boot.

At that moment one of the cowboys ran up to Buck and shouted, "Don't shoot me, Sheriff, I ain't heeled."

Buck shoved him aside and said, "Get a gun or get to running, Holder. This dance has started." The man turned and tore through the door of the cantina.

Buck said, "Go on, Billy. Just follow Brushy Bill."

Billy's eyes flicked back and forth over the lawmen. He cocked his revolver. So did Ortega.

Those clicks were shattering in the brief silence.

Doc thought, *This is not going to end well.*

The fight opened around him with blinding speed. Ike Gore threw open his coat and shouted, "I ain't armed! I ain't armed!" He then reached over his saddle to make another grab for his rifle. Doc gave him both barrels in the side, under his right arm. Ike screamed, staggered into the street, and collapsed groaning against the hitching rail in front of the cantina.

Buck shot Ortega in the stomach at the same time Billy fired at Buck. Billy missed. Cherokee Jim shot Billy in the chest, knocking him back against the side wall of the cantina, just as Buck hit the boy in his shooting arm. Billy slumped down the wall, picked up his revolver with his left hand, and continued firing.

Doc tossed aside the empty shotgun and drew his Colt. Ortega had stumbled into the street in front of Clanton's office, trying to use his own jumpy horse as cover. As the horse bolted, Ortega shouted, "I got you now, old man!" He raised his bone handled Colt toward Doc.

Doc said, "I think not," and shot him in the chest, dropping him.

The boy got off two more shots left handed before running dry. He hit the Major in the leg, dropping him, then put one along Cherokee Jim's back.

Ortega rose to a sitting position and put a bullet through Doc's holster. It burned a furrow along his hip. Major Lang, also sitting, shot Ortega in the chest just as Buck shot him in the side of his head.

The street was filled with smoke but it was suddenly quiet. A Mexican came from the cantina and took the pistol from Billy Gore, slumped against the wall.

"Help me load it, Pablo," the boy muttered. "My right arm ain't working. I keep dropping it . . ."

The Mexican said, "No, *Muchacho,* it's all finished now."

The boy said, "Well, Pablo . . ." then fell over to the side.

Doc cocked his Colt and limped toward Ortega.

"You all right, Doc?" Buck had a revolver in each hand and was checking off the enemy.

"No, Buck, that breed shot me and I mean to make sure he's finished."

"He's finished, Doc. I put one in his brain." Officer Beman stepped into the street and approached Buck. "I must arrest you, Watson."

Buck said, "Not today, Beman. You caused this. You get away from me and stay away."

He turned to his deputies. "Y'all all right?"

Cherokee Jim said, "No, hell no, we ain't all right. The major took at least one in the leg, Doc said he's hit, and I'm shot in the back. You ain't hit?"

Buck said, "I don't think so. You see any blood?"

Doc said, "You appear to be clean." He finished reloading his Colt and lifted Major Lang to his feet. "I'm going in that cantina to check my wound and get out of the open. I suggest you each join me. Come along, Major."

Doc was amazed that he could again breathe normally and speak calmly. The fight was over in less than thirty seconds with about thirty shots fired, and Buck was the only person unscratched. Three dead bandits and three wounded lawmen.

Buck picked up Doc's shotgun. "You need help, Jim?"

Cherokee Jim said, "My backbone hurts like hell, but I can walk."

Buck said, "Then it ain't busted. Hold on a minute. Pablo — is Brushy Bill still in there?"

"*Si, Senor.* He's hiding under the bar. He ask me for a gun, but I don't got one."

Inside, Buck put Brushy Bill on his face in the middle of the floor.

"Lay there like the dog you are," Buck said. "But you itch, just forget about scratching or you join your three dead partners outside."

Doc said, "Cherokee Jim, get out of your coat and shirt while I look at the Major's leg."

Cherokee Jim began to undress. He said, "I will, but I got to tell you, I don't think much of this street fighting business. Standing in the open, everybody blazing away, bullets going every which way? No rocks or

303

trees for cover? No thank you. You English can keep it, if you like it."

Major Lang muttered, "*Gnau.* Exactly. I am not English, but I don't like it either. Is better if different sides wear different clothes. Different colors. In the armies, we do this. It helps us to kill each other."

Doc said, "Major, you'll be fine. Billy's thirty-eight went right through your calf, and there's no cloth missing from your pants. Jim, let's look at you."

Another of young Billy's bullets had chipped Cherokee Jim's spine as it made a neat cut across his back.

Doc whistled. "A half inch difference and you'd be paralyzed, Jim. You are one lucky Cherokee."

"Being so lucky, how come I'm not home with my wife and babies? And what about you? How lucky did you get, Doc?"

Doc shucked his gun belt and dropped his pants to find a forty-five caliber groove along his boney left flank. He said, "Pablo, let's have some strong whiskey to put on these nicks and scratches. Then we'll hobble to the barbershop for some clean linen or plasters to patch us up."

Buck had been squatting beside Brushy Bill Holder, having a quiet talk. He stood and said, "Sounds good, Doc. Then if you and Jim can ride, young Mister Holder there is right eager to take us to where the cows and money is hid."

CHAPTER THIRTY-FOUR

Mary Johnson

Mary Johnson put the last of the bags of dirty laundry in the wagon, then used her apron to mop the sweat from her shiny black face. It was not yet full dark. She knew it would be a while before Sergeant Oregano Jones showed up to drive her back to Sweetwater. It was only a couple of miles, not a bad walk if you weren't carrying several bags of soldiers' clothing.

She sat on the rear stoop of the barracks and lit a pipe. This building was where the sergeants and corporals slept. A few yards away was one of the longer barracks where the other Buffalo Soldiers stayed. Privates. 'Enlisted men' is what Oregano called them. Said him and the older soldiers in his building was 'noncoms,' whatever that was.

Corporal Willie Jackson came out and took his hat off. "Evening, Miz Johnson. I'm heading over to sing a little with the boys next door. Why don't you join us? I bet your voice would be a powerful help to us."

Mary shook her head. She'd tried singing once while she was a Kioway prisoner, and they had beat her bad. Got a headache now, just thinking about singing, even though she loved it back before she was took prisoner, back twelve years ago. Back then, a sharp-looking buck like Willie Jackson woulda been trying to get her to go do something besides singing. Them Kioway had used her hard, and she had grown old quick.

"No, Mister Jackson, you go ahead on. I'll set here and listen. Got to be ready to hop on the wagon and scoot, the very minute Sergeant Jones shows up. Tell them boys hello for me, and tell 'em their clothes'll be ready late tomorrow." *And tell them to kill some Kioways for me whenever they can,* she thought.

"Yassum. Oregano, he still be talking wid the white folks. He be along pretty soon."

"The white folks? Oh — you mean the officers."

"Yassum. But he won't be long. Good night then, Miz Johnson."

Two more corporals spoke as they stepped past her heading for the privy and then the singing.

She was left again to her thoughts, which were always jumbled and often angry. Life had been hard before the war as a slave, but she'd jumped the broom with Britt Johnson and they had some sweet babies and the old man who owned 'em weren't too bad.

Then come the black times, when she was captive and babies was killed 'cept for Cherry, and it took Britt so long to find her and bring her home. She shoulda been happy then, but she had trouble letting go of the anger.

Britt thought she shoulda been proud of him, making all those trips up into the Territory to find her and get her back. And him getting freed, and starting the hauling business and hiring other niggers and all. And it did get some better, but there weren't a single chance Britt would ever understand what she went through. He'd say he wanted to hear it but she knew he really didn't and the black rage would come over her and she couldn't talk. Not about that.

Still, things got better, slow, and Cherry was a delight. Mary got some work and Britt's business prospered and even white folks treated him with some respect. She liked that and resented it, all at the same time.

And then the Kioway caught Britt on the

stage road, six years ago. Killed him and his two men and his mules, took all freight and burned all three wagons. Wiped them out. Talk about dark times.

White folks said she should feel proud, 'cause Nigger Britt put up some kind of a fight. Proud? Try that as a dirt poor nigger widow, on the Texas Frontier with a baby in the winter of '71.

Be proud, they said, but didn't nobody do nothing to help, 'cept Junebug and Buck Watson. She was at rock bottom, lower than snake droppings for the second time in her life and here come those total strangers to save her and her baby. Every time she thought of it she smiled and filled up with thankfulness and sometimes cried.

She wasn't good with words but even if she was she'd probably have trouble explaining why she could be thankful to them and still resentful of Britt. Yeah, he saved her too, but he shoulda never let 'em take her and the children in the first place. And then he let 'em take him.

The rage built again. More than any other feeling, 'cept her love for Cherry, she hated the Kioway. She never saw any way she'd get any revenge, but then one night not long back she'd stumbled on a Kioway brave passed out on the short trail between Camp

Elliott and Sweetwater. He was old and a drunk but she was pretty sure he was one called Hump, and he'd been one of them, up in them Kioway camps.

She'd put her foot on his neck and took her long thin filet knife and jammed it in his ear and twisted it. Scrambled his brains good. Next day when he's found, folks thought some farmer had murdered him for revenge. They weren't far wrong, and she still carried old Hump's Kioway war hatchet or tommyhawk or whatever it's called, stuck in her belt and hid up under her apron.

That was another memory that sometimes let her smile.

Her smile disappeared when she noticed how far the moon had moved since she sat down. Where was Oregano Jones? Old White Buffalo, as the Indians called him. And white folks called him Whitey, and he ain't as black as me, but he is dark. Go figure. Had to be his white hair and mustache, but what kind of name was Oregano, anyways? She asked him did it come from the Bible but he said no, it was something you put on food to spice it up a little. Light and spicy, like him, he said, and they'd both laughed.

Most nights she'd be looking forward to the ride to Sweetwater and some of Oregano Jones' spicy business. He'd pull that wagon into a gully and they'd make a bed of them laundry bags and then grind a little coffee.

Not tonight. Talk around town was that Brushy Bill Holder was back nearby and looking to pay back Buck Watson for wiping out the Ortega gang and getting back them stolen cows. And money. Mary Johnson wanted to get back home and get off the streets and help Junebug keep Buck inside too.

Sergeant Oregano Jones finally showed, mumbling something about "dumb-ass lieutenants," but he'd heard rumors too and was jumpy the whole way to Sweetwater. Wasn't gonna be no coffee grinding tonight.

As they got to the edge of the town, Oregano braked the wagon and jumped down. "You keep the wagon here tonight, Mary. Bring the clean stuff back in it tomorrow. You can get the mules put up, right?"

"I used to be married to a freighter. I reckon I've handled more mules than most men. What you gonna do?"

"I'll walk back, Mary. I got my pistol." He patted the Richards Conversion on his belt, and he was gone.

Mary parked the wagon behind her laundry shed and led the mules into the O.C. Corral. As she closed the gate she heard Buck Watson say good night to Pablo at his cantina. The sheriff must be finishing his rounds, she figured. She decided to cut through the new building that was getting built and meet Buck as he turned the corner toward his office.

She stepped carefully through the new construction, watching for nails in boards, but froze when a match flared ahead of her. A man was there kneeling behind a stack of lumber, a shotgun resting on the stack. Brushy Bill Holder.

As stupid as he's evil, she thought. Laying in ambush for the sheriff, and so scared he has to light up a smoke.

The clatter of approaching boots on the wooden walkway caused Holder to drop the smoke and grab the shotgun. It was already cocked, so the clatter of Buck's boots might have been the last thing Brushy Bill ever heard. Probably, though, it was that crunch as Mary Johnson sunk her Kioway hatchet deep into his skull.

More than Kioways, she thought, I hate anybody trying to mess with my Mister Buck or Miz Junebug. I just won't stand for it.

CHAPTER THIRTY-FIVE

Striker

Striker shook his head and said, "I do not understand this, Weasel. Dobey and Boss Melton want us to travel with them back to the Lodge Pole River country, and this would be a good thing, but Meotzi says she is staying here."

"I have talked to her about this," Weasel said. "She feels it is too soon for Yellow Bird. And Isaac wants her to stay, and be his woman."

The two men were sharing a pipe, sitting on the creek bank in front of Isaac's store.

Striker slapped his leg. "His woman? Who has waited for her for eight summers, while she waited for a husband who turned her out? Me, that is who, not some white storekeeper who has only known her since her husband was killed. He has turned her head with food and trinkets . . ."

Weasel smiled. "And medicine, and a nice

dry cabin, and clothes, and a gentle touch. No, he is no warrior like you, my son, but he has much to offer."

Striker stood and stared at the offending cabin. "Maybe I will just kill him. Let her see how much he has to offer, with a third eye in his forehead from my pistol."

"You will only make her hate you, Striker, and it will change nothing. Meotzi is not a woman you can marry. I would not allow it, even if you wanted to have half-wit children."

Striker yanked Weasel to his feet. "What are you saying, you old fool? Do not think you can make sport with me because you are my father."

Weasel took Striker's face in his hands. "I make no sport. I know how much you care for Meotzi, and it is natural. But you can not marry. She is your sister."

"What? What are you . . . ? My mother did not . . ."

"No. Not your mother. But I was close with her mother too. And her mother's husband, Chief Little Rock, well, he was always going hunting and to peace councils, and . . ."

Striker shouted, "Why have you not told me before?"

Weasel shrugged. "She was married be-

314

fore, and she was waiting for Creeping Panther. Now that he is dead, I am telling you. Think of it this way, son — you have not lost a possible wife. You have gained a sister. And one you do not have to feed."

Striker sat down again and pounded both sides of his head with his fists. "I do not think you are the right person to be talking about family things." He turned suddenly toward Weasel. "But have you told Meotzi of this?"

Weasel said, "No. Why should I? This man Isaac is not one of my children."

Dobey

The little convoy closed in on Deadwood late the following day. Dobey decided that he, Boye and Melton would accompany the muleskinner and his son into Deadwood, while the rest of his party would set up camp well off the trail. And stay out of sight until they returned, with or without Hickok.

As they rode away from the camp, Melton gave Dobey one of his rare smiles. "So, you're of a mind that a Darky, four Injins, and a make-believe priest might not fit in here just yet?"

Dobey grinned back. "What I've heard of this place, we're liable to have to shoot our way out. No point drawing attention, mak-

315

ing ourselves more of a target."

John Boye looked back at the camp. "And I'm thinking Bear and the priest might be fine going in there with us, but them Cheyenne? I'm right tense with them me ownself. For all I knows, they was shooting at me a bare five weeks back. And me at them."

Dobey said, "I need Bear and the preacher man back there in case some miners stumble on 'em. Might be they can talk their way out of a fight. As for the other, what happened up on the Little Bighorn, you're probably right. I just don't know what to do about it. We was pretty tight with those two warriors before Custer ran over them, back on the Washita."

"What you do is you let it go," said Melton. "It's like this. Both sides did what they was supposed to do. They had you bad out-numbered, so they won. But y'all held 'em off, even though you was bad out-numbered. No shame either side, kind of like back in the war. Main thing now is we needs to get home, and like Dobey said back at that store, if we run into a passel of Sioux or Cheyenne, we gonna be happy we got these three Cheyenne with us. Might just save our sorry butts."

"True," said Dobey. "And besides, it ain't like they killed Custer or something."

They followed Deadwood Creek to the muddy main street of Deadwood. The muleskinner and his son pulled their wagon up in front of a hardware store, and told Dobey to try asking about Hickok among the many bars.

Melton grinned and said, "You think so?"

They pulled up in front of a dance hall at Number Six Main. As they tied off, a small group of men came out of the building and stood not five feet from them, arguing. Four men appeared to be gamblers but the fifth was none other than Crooked-Nose Jack McCall, the drunk from the river-boat.

Boye drew his .45, held it down by his leg, and nodded to McCall. McCall frowned but showed no sign of recognition, as the gamblers railed at him.

"You got back yestiddy, and you ain't done nothing?"

"You played cards with him, and didn't shoot?"

McCall said, "I rode like hell from Fort Pierre, didn't wait for no ox-train or nothing, to get here and get it done but the timing just won't right. Too many of his friends was there."

"Well, he's over there in Number Ten right now. Been playing for three hours. Go do what you been paid for."

McCall said, "Don't fret on it. I said I would, and I will. Just don't let 'em hang me." He stepped past Dobey and marched into the street.

Boye said, "I told you he wouldn't remember us. He was cross-eyed drunk the whole trip."

Melton said, "Well, he was surely cross-eyed. He just walked into a horse. Let's go get a drink and see does anybody know where Hickok is."

And that's where I came in.

CHAPTER THIRTY-SIX

I rode with Dobey Walls and Jimmy Melton back during the war, with Terry's Texas Rangers. My daddy was the regimental chaplain, and I sort of became the regimental historian. My name is William Frederick Skipper. I'm called Buddy.

When the Eighth Texas was about to surrender and the commander cut us loose, Dobey and Melton set out for Texas cross-country. My daddy and my brother Marcus and I lit out for Wilmington, over on the North Carolina coast. Thought maybe we'd catch a boat to Texas, maybe Galveston, save us a lot of riding. That just didn't happen.

Daddy got pulled into running an 'all girls' school, and Marcus and I wound up working on tugboats on the Cape Fear River. Wilmington was the last Confederate port to fall and that got it noticed in the shipping business, so the port's business picked up pretty fast. But I missed my writing.

After several years I let go of tug-boating and signed on with the local paper. That was fun but it barely paid the bills. And that's when I noticed the dime novels, and first heard of Wild Bill Hickok.

I'd often thought of writing the history of Terry's Texas Rangers, but there didn't appear to be nearly as much interest in that as there was everywhere about James Butler 'Wild Bill' Hickok, so I resolved to write about him first.

I convinced my editor to let me go in search of Wild Bill and the Real West. He said he'd pay going rate for items of interest and that if I got enough on Hickok for a real book, he'd produce it. Two days later I was heading west.

Six months later I'd scoured the cow towns and got a lot of backstory on Hickok but kept missing him. I lost a lot of time doing odd jobs for food.

I'd even found the graves of my two Ranger heroes, Dobey and Melton, on Boot Hill at Hays City, Kansas. And I'd stood in the saloon where Hickok had been jumped by two Seventh Cavalry soldiers. Where he'd shot himself loose and escaped.

In July 1876 I learned the Seventh Cavalry

had lost a least a third of its force along with its commander, a Yankee colonel named Custer, up in the Black Hills and at the same time found that Hickok was in the Black Hills himself. In a new mining town called Deadwood. A week later I was with a mule train to go see the place with such a magical name.

On August 2, 1876, I arrived mid-afternoon, and rode slowly down Main Street, soaking in the jumble and bustle. I intended to get a feel for the place, get a bath and a meal, and write down my first impressions all before searching for Mister Hickok.

Mid-way down Main, three riders ahead of me pulled left and tied off near a group of men on the boardwalk. One of the new arrivals drew an Army Colt and held it down along his leg.

I thought, *First day in Deadwood and I'm going to witness a killing. How appropriate.* It didn't happen. Not then.

The group on the boardwalk broke up. Four of them went inside a saloon and the fifth stepped into the street and walked right into my horse. He was completely wall-eyed, possibly drunk and certainly distracted. He muttered, "Why don't you watch where you're going," to a large bay standing stock still, and I remember thinking that he was so ugly that only a blind mother could love him.

He stepped around us and continued across the street and I returned my attention to the three men who'd preceded me into town. The potential assassin returned his pistol to its holster, and only then did I really look at his companions.

If I hadn't known they were dead and buried, I'd have sworn they were Captain Dobey Walls and Sergeant Major Jimmy Melton. I tied off and followed them into the saloon, half expecting to walk into a gunfight.

What it was, though, was a reunion.

Chapter Thirty-Seven

I stepped into the darkened room, which turned out to be a dance hall, barely lit by kerosene lanterns. I moved to the right to clear the doorway and to give my eyes a chance to adjust, and of course I jostled a sporting man. He spilled some beer, I said I was terribly sorry, and he took issue with my heritage and parentage.

Things went downhill from there. I didn't like being called a "clumsy rebel bastard," but since I still couldn't see who or how many I was up against, my options were limited. There were three or four silhouettes between me and the bar, and maybe three more to the left of the door.

The one in front of me shoved me back into the light of the door, and called me a stupid rebel. I believe to this day if he had left out the 'rebel' part, I'd have died right there. They had me fully lit in the doorway, I had to do something, and I couldn't see them, but that 'rebel' business upset several other folks. Praise the Lord.

As it was, there was a rash of clicks as the three men to my left drew and cocked their revolvers and moved up beside me. I was pleased and relieved to see their pistols were pointing at the sporting crowd. The biggest one of my new-found friends said, "Say what, you Yankee asshole?"

There was a flurry of apologies from the sporting crowd — "Didn't mean no rudeness," "Just joking," "He's drunk. Don't pay him no mind," "Jesus, Barker, you coulda got us killed," — but the big man beside me said, "Keep 'em covered, Dobey. I want 'em outa here and gone. Don't want no sneak shots in the dark from no back-shooting gamblers."

He pushed me aside and waved the four gamblers outside, then followed them out. He sure looked like Jimmy Melton, only heavier.

I said, "Dobey? Dobey Walls?"

The smaller man stepped up close and said, "My God. Buddy Skipper?"

Melton came back in at that moment, and there was a whole bunch of back-slapping and talking over one another, and introductions all around. Finally somebody said, "What the hell are you doing here?"

When I told them, Dobey said, "We're here to find him too."

Some local yahoo who'd been listening in said, "Well, if y'all wants to talk to Hickok, you'd best slide on over to Number Ten pretty fast. Across the street. Them gamblers just sent Jack McCall over there to shoot him."

We headed over, double quick, and pushed in just as it happened. There was a bar along the right wall, and about halfway down it, four men sat at a table. The gambler I took to be Hickok sat almost facing me, with his back sort of to the bar. A man came out of the gloom in the back of the saloon, pointed a pistol and shouted, "Take that!"

I still have a crystal-clear picture in my head of it all. The same cross-eyed, ugly young man I'd seen in the street, the smoke billowing around the gambler's head, the hole blossoming under his eye, the blood spray just as I heard the bang. The player across from the shot man shouting, "Damn!" and grabbing his wrist, the shot man flopping face down on the table, then sliding off onto the floor.

The shooter waved his pistol at those of us who had crowded in and shouted, "Get out! Get back out!"

Everyone turned back on us and drove us

back onto the boardwalk. Just as I was pushed out, I saw the cross-eyed shooter point his revolver at the bartender and snap the hammer at him. I'm sure it was a misfire, and then the shooter fled for the back door.

Melton saw it too. He yelled at Dobey and Boye to go 'round back to the right, then said "C'mon," and led me to the left.

We got back there first, and McCall snapped a misfire at us. We ducked, and then he popped a cap at Dobey and Boye. They ducked too, but before any of us could shoot him he threw down his pistol, an old Starr cap and ball Navy, and said, "Don't shoot. I surrender. He killed my brother."

I think Melton would have shot him anyway, but several gamblers rushed up to arrest the wall-eyed scoundrel and haul him away to safety.

So now you know why you've never seen the book called, "*The Definitive Life of James B. Hickok,* by William F. Skipper, as told by Wild Bill." I never wrote it, as I never spoke to him. It's possible I saw him alive for a fraction of a moment, but I couldn't even swear to that. I can attest to the fact that he was deader than a nail when his face hit that table; he uttered no assurances to his mother or bride or partners with his last breath.

With McCall arrested, we rode back to the camp where the rest of Dobey's party waited. I was introduced to Shelly, Bear, Cranky Bear Woman, Striker, Weasel, and 'Father' Mike O'Hanley, and then the reminiscing began again, with Shelly translating in Cheyenne to make it easy for the two warriors.

At some point, Dobey said, "So, the man we were hunting, Penn, he was killed up there at the Little Bighorn. John Boye confirmed it. His boss was called Red and we been told he was killed by Comanches down in the Llano Estacado. We had some Pinkertons looking for us over a stolen payroll, but those fake graves you saw in Hays seem to have caused 'em to give up on us."

"Yeah," said Melton, "And so the one thing might still be hanging over us is a town marshal, who's way off his reservation, but might still be looking for us. I knocked a bunch of his teeth out."

"Right," said Dobey. "A renegade named Fetterman."

"I think that man is dead." Shelly spoke, as matter of fact as you please, and never looked up from her cooking. Her statement apparently astounded Dobey, Bear, and Melton.

"What the hell?" said Dobey.

"Come again?" said Bear.

Melton said, "Who told you such a thing, girl?"

"Bobby Joe Jackson. The man I stabbed, and you tied him to a tree near Fort Worth. When I shifted him so he could see downhill, he said, 'This all started when we killed that durn Marshal Fetterman.' I thought that was a funny name so I asked him what he said, and he said it again. Marshal Fetterman, he said. It was just before the bear bit off his head, and almost tore off my teat."

Melton shook his head and yelled, "And how come you ain't tole us this before?"

Shelly frowned at him. "Because I never heard his name again until now. And you never asked me or even told me about him. And I cannot see into your head, even if you shout."

"Well, well then, where was Bear?"

"Off getting his head kicked in by your horse."

It was clear to me at that moment that there was a story here, much better than the life of Wild Bill.

McCall was tried and found not guilty the following day. Clearly that was a jury of Mc-

Call's peers. He was picked up later in a better town, tried again, and hanged. Couldn't have happened to a better man.

■ ■ ■ ■

1889

■ ■ ■ ■

CHAPTER THIRTY-EIGHT

I can't tell you much about that long trip from Deadwood, Dakota Territory, to Canadian Fort, Texas in August 1876. I spent the entire time mining the memories of my fellow travelers. I filled up a large notebook, bought another somewhere in Colorado Territory, and then filled it too.

Those two notebooks were combined with my historical records from the war to form the foundation for my previous two novels, *No Good Like It Is* and *Dog Soldier Moon,* as well as for this piece you are now reading. It was only a foundation, as I have now spent over ten years traveling, searching, researching, and editing, in an attempt to make the story of this community, this family, into something readable.

My efforts were made manageable by two utterly despicable acts of selfishness on my part. In 1868 I married an older woman in Wilmington, N.C. I did not love her. In

1875, I left her, though I did not leave her starving.

She was the only child of a widower who was not well. He did own 800 acres of bottom land along the Cape Fear River, unfit to grow anything but mosquitos and hogs. He had another 150 acres in corn, which fed his hogs and the local bootlegging industry. By 1875 he was wealthy. And very sick, and all my bride wanted to do was care for her dear, poor daddy. I still believe that was because he was the only person in the entire universe who would listen to her prattle for sixteen hours a day. A stroke had left him speechless.

Cornelia and I had no children. I don't know if that was because she was barren or if she 'took steps' because she didn't want any competition in the noise area. Possibly it was just that she never stopped chattering until she fell asleep, which provided me a welcome lack of opportunity. I never said she was desirable. Or interesting. 'Available' is a good word, and she could cook.

She was also generous. She sent drafts a time or two while I searched for Wild Bill, but then her poor, dear, speechless, rich daddy died in early 1877. Of boredom, I suspect, but at any rate I received a handsome sum with a note from her attorney to the effect that the payments would continue so long as I did not file for a divorce.

I was now a gentleman journalist, and happily married for the first time in my life.

Correspondence with my brother back in Wilmington explained it all. Cornelia had taken up with a childhood friend, a spinster librarian, and needed our marriage to defuse any scandal. Unable to converse at the library, the spinster was apparently perfectly content with Cornelia's nonstop babble after hours.

Cornelia. Bless her heart, I hope she's as happy as all of her hogs, cavorting and multiplying down in her bottom land. I just hope she lives forever, or at least outlives me. She has provided me the time and wherewithal to discover and pursue my dream, which is the story of Dobey and the Boss. And pursue it I have, for thirteen years now.

That was August of '76. The next thirteen years didn't exactly fly by, but we managed to survive them. That outcome wasn't always clear; there were snakebites, blizzards, fires, droughts, births, and even a few gunfights. And tornados. Don't forget them.

Bat Masterson recovered from his wound and moved to Dodge City. Dobey, Melton, Cherokee Jim, and even I rode with the

Frontier Battalion of the Texas Rangers on occasion, while Bear spent even more time with the Tenth Cavalry of Buffalo Soldier fame. 'Padre' Mike O'Hanley established a church and a school at Canadian Fort, and the rodeo came to town.

Ostrich Ranch became big enough to sustain horrible losses in several blizzards and yet remain one of the preeminent cattle empires in the Panhandle. Willi and Lang purchased '73 Winchesters for Dobey's ranger company back in '75 when most rangers were equipped with single-shot Sharps conversion carbines and Colt .45's. In '78, when Colt finally brought out a .44-40 version of the Peacemaker, Willi ordered them for Dobey's men as companion guns for their Winchesters, so they could get by with one kind of ammunition.

There were hundreds of terribly interesting events such as these in our growing community during those years, but that's another story, as none of those news items had anything to do with the story of Honey's missing gun.

The story. I am immersed in it. Consumed by it. I've had to guess at much, but what is shocking is how much I've confirmed by being free to travel and bother people with lots of digging.

For example, the missing pistol itself. Honey's superstition gun. Buck Watson's father saw it in Red's hand when he killed those Pinkerton's in Santa Fe back in '68. One of the Pinkertons had even called out the serial number before Red killed him and took it back.

For the longest time, we figured the gun had been lost to the Comanches that supposedly killed Red over in the Staked Plains, but my trip to Santa Fe to meet Buck's parents had yielded more than one nugget.

The jailer informed me that the man they knew as Robbins was released and put on the northeast stage with no coat, no weapon, and two dollars of traveling money. But I found the driver of that stage, then a retired auxiliary constable, and he said that same man flashed that pistol in the stage to Dodge, showing everyone the 'triple-nickel' serial number. He also had a slicker and cash, and was the prime suspect in the death of the station master at Twenty-Mile Station, but 'Robbins' had then disappeared.

Well, Robbins had been dead for years before that, along with the other junior members of Red's gang. That leaves Penn. How'd he get the pistol from Red? Maybe from Consuela, who'd worked for Red in Silver City. My guess is as good as yours.

As time passed, so did the reluctance of Striker and Weasel to talk about the Little Bighorn. They never owned up to killing the Custer brothers — I got that from Meotzi on a later trip to see her — but they did admit to shooting a civilian scout that day, and taking that pistol from a saddle pouch near his body. And they said Meotzi identified him as Penn, a man she had hated for years.

And they told me they had given the pistol to Meotzi because of some mystical significance, which they chose not to explain.

The next day after I heard that, I was heading for Izaac's Store, way up near Deadwood. I paid Shelly and Bear to accompany me, since they'd been there before. And they seemed lonely; their oldest son Black Dog was a corporal in the Tenth Cavalry, a proud buffalo soldier, decorated for several engagements against the Apache. Their youngest boy, James Melton Weathers, was seventeen and was known as 'Jimmy M' on the rodeo circuit. He was away often winning cash and animals. Bear and Shelly seemed happy at the invitation to travel.

Everyone liked to travel with me because I was a good listener and, like Melton frequently pointed out, I had more money than brains.

It was May of 1889 and it was another long journey. Like so many others it produced a wealth of filler information for me, and another dead end.

Meotzi and Izaac seemed genuinely happy together and were right liquid with joy to see Bear and Shelly again. By that I mean they damn near wet themselves.

Me they weren't so sure of. Even thirteen years after Custer's death, most Sioux and Cheyenne were not comfortable admitting to any whites that they were anywhere near the Little Bighorn that day in June 1876. You ask them, they'd say they'd been hunting elk in Canada or enjoying hot baths over on the Yellowstone. Couldn't exactly remember where they'd picked up that trapdoor carbine, or that Cavalry model Colt .45 or that old gray hat with the crossed sabers on it.

Fortunately for me, Shelly had never been shy about talking and her friendship with Meotzi went back to teenaged days on the Washita, back before Meotzi's first meeting with the Custer family.

By the time I met Meotzi she spoke excellent English, and she soon loosened up. She was a treasure chest. It gave me chill bumps to listen to her describe both fights, the

Greasy Grass and the Lodge Pole River, but most staggering was to learn that two of my closest friends for the last thirteen years had taken part in the deaths of Major Elliot and his men, as well as the Custer brothers.

When I finally felt all right to ask about the Superstition Gun, Meotzi hung her head.

"My son, Yellow Bird, he is now a scout with the White cavalry. He was taken from us for a while and sent to White school. They gave him a White name, John Steele, but they taught him well and he speaks your talk more better than me. I am mostly very proud of him."

She picked up a photograph from the desk beside her and passed it to us. John 'Yellow Bird' Steele was a strikingly handsome twenty-year old who obviously captured the best features of both parents, but no, he does not have a streak of golden hair. Not even a trace.

When Meotzi returned the picture to the desk she sat staring at it silently. Somehow, I knew better than to interrupt. Shelly did not.

"What did he do to shame you?" she said. Shelly was nothing if not direct.

Meotzi teared up and looked out the window.

Izaac patted her arm, then said, "He didn't do nothing to shame nobody. She gave him that little pistol as a luck token. The gun that killed Custer. Yellow Bird carried and protected it for years but last year while he was bathing, a soldier got into his traps. Took the pistol, his watch, his Colt, and his money. Deserted. Went south. Yellow Bird took off after him but only learned that the deserter had got in a fight on a train way south of here. Over cards. Conductor killed him."

"Who got the gun?" I asked.

"Yellow Bird was sure the conductor got it, but he wouldn't own up to it, and Yellow Bird didn't dare speak the gun's history. Last he heard the conductor had gone down El Paso way. Yellow Bird come back and was court-martialed for desertion himself, but since he brought back the deserter's body, they went light on him. Just made him pay for the stolen Colt. But Meotzi can't hardly forgive him for losing that gun."

We stayed for a week, and I nearly filled another notebook, what with Meotzi's stories and all the items I gleaned from Bear and Shelly as we traveled. All of that was good, but I hated losing track of little Number 555.

When we finally got home, we came in on the same train that Brick Walls was getting on, going south to El Paso. We only had time to shake hands and trade best wishes. If I'd known what he was up to, I'd have stayed on that train, but I didn't, and I was travel-weary and so I missed the final chapter of the saga of Honey's gun.

Doesn't seem fair. I was that close.

Brick Walls was Honey's second child; her first was Millie, Dobey's daughter and one of the first females to compete in rodeos, often going head to head with her cousin 'Jimmy M.'

Brick was the rusty-haired illegitimate result of Honey's rape by Red Dodd, back in '68. Brick was now a rising star in the Rangers, following in Dobey's footsteps, so to speak.

The new commander of the Rangers decided to test the 'One riot, one ranger' theory by sending Brick alone to San Isleta down by El Paso to help out some old constable who was in over his head.

It wasn't clear then whether it was to prove the theory with the son of a legend, or because the commander was jealous of Dobey's reputation. It wasn't even in our ranger company's district.

I don't think that matters. What follows is what happened.

CHAPTER THIRTY-NINE

Brick

Brick got his mare off the train in El Paso, then walked her around a while to get her legs back under her after the lurching, lunging ride. A Mexican pointed the way to San Isleta, and he was soon standing in the constable's office.

"So, you the advance guard, sort of?" The constable was a large white-haired lawman named Whitey. Go figure.

"Nossir. I'm all they sent. Why? You expecting an army or something?"

"No, but they is maybe twenty of 'em. I mean, I asked for a section. Figgered y'all might send a squad at least. You ain't joshing me? There ain't ten more out back? I got a copy of my telegraph."

Brick said, "Why don't you just tell me what we're up against, and let's go from there?"

"Hmmph," snorted Whitey. "Well, we had

us a kind of salt dispute a ways back, and some of the damn Mexicans ain't ever felt it was resolved right. Now they's talking about taking back the salt mines, and killing me and the Texans who legally own it. I been kind of penned in here, waiting for support. And the damn government sends me a child. Though you look capable. No offense."

"No offense taken. Where can I talk to these Mexicans?"

"Well," said Whitey, "they mean to pass by here with wagons on the way to the mine in the morning, though I don't know how much talking they'll tolerate."

Brick shrugged. "My daddy used to be a ranger. He always said, 'Just go right at 'em.' How many shotguns you got?"

Next morning when the two Mexican wagons arrived, there were a bunch of hay bales blocking the road. Six wide, three high. Behind them were Whitey, his deputy, and Brick, with six shotguns laying on top of the barricade. And a mess of revolvers and Winchesters.

The lead driver, who was somewhat hung over, said something that sort of translated to, "What the hell?"

Brick said, "*Com esta, Amigos?* Y'all speak

some English, maybe?" He cocked both barrels of his shotgun and pointed them at the lead driver.

"*Si,*" the Mexican said, somewhat tremulously, "A little. *Un poco.*"

"Good," Brick said. "You ain't going past here 'til we're dead. And we figger we can kill most of you afore that happens. But you're first. *Numero uno,* no matter what."

There was some nervous chatter from the exposed Mexicans on the wagons. Finally the leader said, "But, we need salt. Everybody needs salt."

Brick said, "Not if you're dead. Here's the thing. There was this war about this, and y'all lost. You got to pay for the salt now. Shit like this happens. What I think? I think you tell these gringos you ain't gonna buy no more salt from 'em, they'll come down on the price. Can't hurt to try that. Damn sure ain't no good like it is."

After some internal discussion and a lot of staring at those six shotguns, the Mexicans turned and rode back toward the Rio Grande.

Brick said, "Sweet Jesus. You couldn't drive a nail up my ass with a nine pound hammer right now. You got something to drink?"

Whitey said, "I think that was a whole

bunch closer than it seemed. So, who was your daddy?"

"Thomas Walls. Step-daddy, that is."

"Where from?"

"Little town called Canadian Fort, up near Adobe Walls. Of course, folks call him Dobey. And I'm Brick, 'cause of my hair."

Whitey turned to his deputy. "Bill, you follow 'em. Watch and see do they cross over the river and stay there. Me and the ranger is gonna go to Fat Rosie's."

"I know why you're here." Whitey held the shotgun loose and low, not exactly pointing it at Brick. "I just now figgered it out."

Brick turned. "Say what?" The afternoon rainstorm, rare and violent, had finally broken and the two men were crossing from the cantina to Whitey's office.

"You're here to kill me. Pretending like you come to help, and the whole time you're here 'cause your daddy sent you. To kill me."

"You drunk, Whitey? I don't even know my daddy."

"Yeah, you do. Don't try to feed me that stuff. You belong to one of them old Rangers up at Canadian Fort. One of them was named Walls."

Brick squinted at the old lawman with new interest. "It ain't been two hours since

I told you that. One of them old Rangers took me as his own, but he won't my daddy. What do you know about Canadian Fort?"

Whitey cocked both barrels, and brought the gun to his shoulder. "Cut the bullshit, boy, and get ready to die. They sent you to get me 'cause of what we did to their women. They wasn't man enough no more to come themselves?"

Brick was frozen. "What're you saying? What did you do?"

"Aw, like you don't know," Whitey slurred. "Me and the boys was drunk, had a little fun with 'em. They asked for it, then went kind of crazy. Hell, the young one shot me, and the other one set fire to ol' Robbins. We had to put 'em down."

"You didn't kill both of 'em ," Brick spat the words out. "You kilt my granma all right. Left Mama for dead but she weren't. You did leave her carrying me. And I been hoping to find you, you son of a bitch, ever since I's born."

Now Whitey was frozen. "Don't you move. Just hang on here a minute. Are you saying you're . . ."

The barrel of the shotgun wavered for an instant. Brick lunged and pushed it aside with his left as he went for his own pistol, but the shot came from behind Whitey.

Whitey said, "Owww," and grabbed his butt with his left hand, then dropped the shotgun and cupped his groin with his right. As he turned to face his attacker, she fired again. Whitey said, "Rosie? What the hell . . . lemme see that pistol!"

Fat Rosie Rojas lurched toward him in a red satin dress, a fan in one hand, a sawed-off Smith & Wesson in the other. "I tole you, you pig-sticking whore gringo son a bitch, I tole you." She stopped, teetered, went back a step and fired a third time. "You use me badly jus' one more time, I kill you. Didn't I tole you?" She fired again.

The little .32 caliber balls had not knocked Whitey down. He yelled and lunged at her, but that fourth shot took out a knee and he tumbled.

Brick drew and covered her. "Let it go, Fat Rosie. Put it down. I think you've killed him. No, wait, DAMN," he shouted as she fired again, hitting Whitey in the head. The constable convulsed, twisting in short spasms.

Rosie staggered over to the twitching lawman, steadied herself, then wiped the drunken tears with her left sleeve. She spat on Whitey and said, "How'd you like that one in the butt, you pig?" Whitey went limp.

Still sobbing, she turned back to Brick.

She tried to smile through the smeared makeup and pig-like eyes. Brick thought, *The face of a nightmare.*

"I tole him. He shoulda listen to me. You know, he talk, he make people laugh, but he mean, too mean, clean through." Staring straight at Brick, she swung the pistol to her right and fired the last shot into Whitey's back, then tossed the pistol onto his body. "You can have it now, gringo." She went sideways two steps and sat down in the mud.

"This seems to be all of his earthly possessions, Ranger Walls. Not much to show." Harley Gaston was a former Texas Ranger himself. He was also the circuit judge.

Three people were in Whitey's office. Fat Rosie sat beside the desk, drinking coffee and giving up an occasional soft hiccup. Brick sat in Whitey's chair while Judge Gaston leaned on the desk, staring at the dead lawman's treasures. The rumble of the pouring rain was interrupted by a flash of a nearby lightning strike, and two of them jumped as thunder cracked immediately afterward.

"Lord a 'mercy!" said Judge Gaston.

Fat Rosie said, *"Madre de Dios!"* She crossed herself.

Dobey just grinned. "I'm guessing y'all

don't get much of that down here. Go ahead on with your story, Rosie."

"I did tole him," Fat Rosie said again. "He shouldn't have done it."

Brick shook his head. "Yeah, Rosie. You told him. When was that, exactly? He was pretty old to be using women badly."

"Mebbe two year ago. I tole him, never again or I'd kill him."

"Judas Priest, two years ago. And he did it again? When?"

"Mebbe six month ago. That's when I tell myself maybe I use this little *pistola.*"

Judge Gaston picked up the pistol and held it absent-mindedly. "My daddy always said revenge was a meal best enjoyed cold. Well, ain't nobody gonna miss him. What I'm told, he's been shaking down most ever'body. Must've thought you was here to clean things up."

As Brick considered that, he stared at the other items still on the desk. Thirty-one dollars and change, a silver brush, a hasp knife, a .44-40 Remington revolver and holster with silver conchos, and his town constable badge. And another old badge. Brick picked it up.

"Town Marshal," he read. "Mason's Landing. He must of law'd there 'fore he come here. No family? Anybody know?"

The door slammed as Deputy Bill Meinel came in, shaking off the rain. "Naw," he said slapping his hat against his leg. "Not really. He come limping in here maybe fifteen, twenty year ago, messed up with old gunshot wounds. Afore my time, but ol' Creech Jeffords, used to run the stable, he told me about it. Said Whitey had kind of rusty hair, which turned white almost overnight. Probably how he got his name."

Judge Gaston winked at Brick and said, "You reckon?"

The deputy nodded. "I mean his ever'day name, of course. His real name was Dodd. Christopher Columbus Dodd. He run a eatin' place up in Silver City afore it was called Silver City. He'd drink and talk about a woman up north, somewhere. Long time ago. French, he said. Give him a little storekeeper pistol. 'For services rendered,' he'd always say. Meant he'd done something good for her, I reckon. Anyways, he had to leave it when he skipped outta Silver City. Said it had a peculiar serial number, and was always bad luck. He didn't mind losing it none." He picked up the pistol as the Judge put it down. "Must have been just like this here one. See the number on it? Five-fifty-five. Ain't that bad luck?"

"Five-fifty-five?" Brick swallowed hard

and took the pistol. "Whoa. Where'd you get this pistol, Rosie? Did you get it from Whitey?"

"No, I didn't take no gun from him. A railroad man give me that gun when he didn't have no money to pay for his fun. He was gonna bring me some money and get it back, but Whitey got drunk and beat him bad and ran him outta town."

"Well, I don't know how that railroad man got it, but that there was my Mama's gun, and this ain't the first time old Whitey was shot with it. Boss Melton always said it was bad luck, and Papa Dobey called it the Superstition Gun. Heard about it all my life. And here it saves my life."

The judge said, "Maybe it wasn't ever a bad gun, except for bad people."

Brick shook his head. "I just wish it could talk. I'd pay good money to hear that story." He stood and walked to the window. "It's near too much to take in. Me and Papa Dobey been looking for this one man, my real daddy, for nigh on forever. Looking to kill him too, and about given up on it. Heard he was kilt by Comanches, but had no proof on it. Then, of all the Rangers in Texas, I get sent to help out this old codger, and we help each other, and then he turns on me and gets kilt by a distressed whore.

353

With my Mama's pistol. Go figure."

Deputy Meinel shook his head. "Ain't no way you could make somethin' like that up."

Outside, bright sunlight blazed suddenly as the rain stopped and the clouds parted. Brick stared out the window and said, "Got to be a rainbow in all this, somewheres. My Mama does like a rainbow."

ABOUT THE AUTHOR

Married in 1960, **McKendree R. (Mike) Long III** and his wife Mary have two married daughters, four grandchildren, and a great-grandson. He holds a BS in Business Administration, and is a gun enthusiast. He's a member of the SCV, DCV, NRA, WWA, MWSA, SASS, VFW, and Sertoma. He is often found on Seabrook Island, S.C.

His first novel, *No Good Like It Is,* is a winding tale of violence, tolerance, and changing racial acceptance. In it, two hard-bitten Confederate cavalrymen barely survive the Civil War, riding with the famed Eighth Texas Cavalry. They then must struggle home to the Texas Panhandle, while accumulating enough misfits and strays to populate a small village. This rowdy historical fiction is filled with rich characters, both real and should-have-been. The sequel, *Dog Soldier Moon,* was published in December 2011. It centers on Custer's attack on a friendly Cheyenne camp in November 1868. Both novels are solidly based in history, and are available through Amazon, Kindle, over 100 Indie bookstores, and the author at www.mckendreelong.com.

Mike has also had three short stories published, including *Chouteau's Crossing* which was finalist for a prestigious Spur Award in Short Fiction given out at the 2014 Western Writers of America Sacramento convention. In September 2014 he finished his fourth novel, *Brodie,* a Western of pure fiction.

The employees of Thorndike Press hope you have enjoyed this Large Print book. All our Thorndike, Wheeler, and Kennebec Large Print titles are designed for easy reading, and all our books are made to last. Other Thorndike Press Large Print books are available at your library, through selected bookstores, or directly from us.

For information about titles, please call:
   (800) 223-1244

or visit our Web site at:
   http://gale.cengage.com/thorndike

To share your comments, please write:
   Publisher
   Thorndike Press
   10 Water St., Suite 310
   Waterville, ME 04901

[5]